BCE 9172

P9-AGI-891

WITHDRAWN
UTSA LIBRARIES

PHANTOMS

a collection of stories

also by Barton Midwood

BODKIN

PHANTOMS

a collection of stories

by BARTON MIDWOOD

 E. P. Dutton & Co., Inc., New York 1970

Copyright © 1970, 1969, 1968, 1967, 1966, by Barton Midwood
All rights reserved. Printed in the U.S.A.

First Edition

No part of this publication may be reproduced or transmitted
in any form or by any means, electronic or mechanical, including
photocopy, recording, or any information storage and retrieval
system now known or to be invented, without permission in writing
from the publisher, except by a reviewer who wishes to quote brief
passages in connection with a review written for inclusion in a
magazine, newspaper, or broadcast.

Published simultaneously in Canada by Clarke, Irwin & Company
Limited, Toronto and Vancouver

Library of Congress Catalog Card Number: 72-108893

Some of the stories in this volume originally appeared in
The Paris Review, The Transatlantic Review, Esquire, and *Cavalier.*

LIBRARY
University of Texas
At San Antonio

Contents

Contents

PHANTOMS

a collection of stories

One's Ship

I am up to my calves in the sea, the very beginnings of the sea which stretches before me out to the edge of the sky. My ship, my tiny ship moored in the shallows, rocks back and forth anxiously, like a schoolboy. The waves lap at its side, the cool waters. Ah, let us go, let us set forth, my ship!

But I am detained. All the women have gathered on the beachhead. We must deal with them, my ship and I. All want to make passage with us. They are shrieking, moaning, imploring. Each woman presents a plaintive convincing case. Each, it is clear from their arguments, deserves beyond the shadow of a doubt to accompany me. They love me, they say. Of course! I am irresistible. My rudder is golden, my sails ample, I have shapely legs. On the beach, with the wind blowing in my thin hair, I make an appealing picture. I am the captain of a noble craft, of everything in fact in sight. I am the only man for miles around. I am needed, that's clear. But how should I take them all, these lovely creatures? There is room for but one companion and frankly I am loath to take anyone beside myself. I am selfish, utterly. The wind blows in my hair. I turn to them and raise my arms for silence. I shall speak. A hush falls. All eyes grow round and soft and fix me tenderly. The tears flow. It is touching. The back of my shirt bellies like a sail.

"Ladies," I say, "I should like to speak to you individually. Form a line!"

They fight for first place. They pull one another's hair. They make an undignified spectacle. At last, however, they are in single file, a long line that runs back from the shore, across the beach, out to the road, and . . . to the ends of the earth for all I know. Nevertheless, I shall give them audience, each one. I must be fair!

I bid the first come forward.

"Yvonne!" I cry. "Come here, my dear. I love you passionately. Let me touch you."

I caress her thighs, she throws her arms around my neck, and we kiss so unconscionably that we fall to the ground and roll in the sand. We have no regard. One forgets oneself. There is nothing to be done.

"Have no fear," I whisper as we stand up and brush the sand from our mouths. "You are the one. I shall take you with me."

She kisses me lightly on the forehead, holding my face in her hands and standing just on her toes. Then she retires to a shady spot beneath a palm and waits. From her purse she takes an orange and sucks it. She stares at me over it from under lowered brows.

"Next!"

Elsa steps forward. She runs at me, leaps into the air, locking her legs around my waist, wraps her arms around my neck, those slender tan arms with the light down, and kisses me precisely on the lips.

"You are the one," I whisper. "Have no fear."

She too retires to a palm and sucks an orange. They have all brought oranges. It must be the season.

Shy and blushing comes Natalie. She looks at the ground. She falls in a faint at my feet. I lift her in my arms and lave her forehead with handfuls of the sea. She comes to.

"Be happy," she says in a swoon. "I am so embarrassed. All these people . . . oh, oh, forgive us. I love you so. You are not in debt to me. I shall always love you. You must take whom you please."

And then she falls to crying, her lips wet with her tears on my neck.

"Natalie," I say, "you are not like the others. I shall take you with me. Have no fear."

Ecstatically she too retires to a palm. She eats an apple however. She is different.

So it goes. Three, four, five days pass in this way—talking, embracing, promising, eating apples and oranges. I have spoken to one and a half billion women—yes! I have counted assiduously. I have promised each one that I will take her with me. It is difficult to say no. How does one say no when one is intoxicated with saying yes? Saying yes is my whiskey. It burns so pleasantly. And after the first few, the rest go down so easily! Yes, yes, yes! It is only no that tastes bitter in my mouth. And what do I care for bitterness? What do I care for . . .

I know. You will say, "He is a fool. He does not know how to handle his affairs. He does not appreciate fully the efficacy of saying no. He is a sensualist and cares for nothing but the moment. He has not a practical vision. He will cause nothing but anguish in this world with his infernal yes."

And so be it! Say it! I know all that! And I care not!

They sit there now, my pretty little one and a half billion; I face them with my hands on my hips. What now? I could make a dash for the ship but they would be brawling on the deck, before I could hoist the mainsail. They would destroy the ship in a moment. I know something about crowds.

I turn my back to them. Bobbing up and down in the sea are the lovely mermaids with the long flowing hair—light green hair, with streaks of blonde that shimmer in the sun. Breasts high and firm, bellies silky, these creatures are not half fish as the mythologies say. Under the surface of the waters, from the waist down, they are womanly, with sleek strong legs. The poets have cunningly perpetrated that half fish business on the public in order to discourage exploitation.

"Ladies," I announce, suddenly, whirling around. "I must test the ship. I must take a brief spin about the harbor. I shall return shortly. And then the chosen one will join me . . ."

This pronouncement seems to disconcert them. There is a sullen suspicious murmur of disapproval. I walk very cautiously to the ship. I make no sudden movement that might alarm them. I walk slowly, slowly, cautiously, like a man who walks past a mad dog. I attempt to make myself invisible. I hold my breath.

The mainsail is up. I push off, I glide . . . glide upon the waters. I am safe, free! I glide, glide! I laugh! I wave my hand-kerchief in farewell! I am safe! Out of touch! The mermaids beckon me with their arms, their heads tilted slightly upward. They burst into a chorus of song—an ethereal song, fathomless and sea-struck. I cannot whistle that tune, but I hear it in my dreams—every note I know. I have heard it, every note, before. Why then can I not whistle it? I am not a bad whistler. In fact, I am rather musical. I know, like the palm of my hand, the music at the bottom of things.

There is a rustling sound below—footsteps coming up the ladder from the hold. A woman climbs on deck. She has a child cradled in her arms and a fierce expression in her eyes. Of course. One hopes beyond hope. There is no escape. One knew it all along. The mermaids make piteous lament! Their song is swallowed in the roar of the sea. There is a storm coming out of the west. There is always a storm coming out of the west; one accepts that. One never examines one's ship carefully enough. One escapes the beach, one escapes half the world, but never looks thoroughly enough into the nooks and crannies of one's own ship.

"The raft," I say. "Take the raft and paddle yourselves back to shore. One is displeased. Do you hear? Displeased!"

Without a word she loosens the chains from the raft and kicks it into the sea.

"The raft!" I cry. "What have you done?"

She says nothing. Her eyes accuse me. One is made to feel guilty by those eyes. And then the child sets to howling. Moreover, the storm is coming out of the west . . . one has set off; one is on one's voyage.

I sit on the deck, hang my hands limply over the edge . . . the mermaids kiss my fingertips. I go on but I know not where I go. A return to the beach is out of the question. I entertain thoughts of pushing the stowaways overboard, but they are tenacious. And then, perhaps, yes, perhaps I need them for ballast. I comfort myself with these thoughts. I contrive reasons for needing them. That is how one's mind works. One has them, one cannot rid oneself easily of them—at least not without committing a heinous crime—so one contrives reasons for needing them. One always needs what one has. If ever one allows oneself to think one does not need what one has, then one is . . .

Under the Mount of Saturn

It's all in the hand—a catastrophe! I found out yesterday. I believe in it. Yes. Why not? I clean the streets, I believe in all sorts of things, it takes a nerve. I don't really clean the streets, that's just an easy way to say it. I don't have anything to do with the streets, in fact. That's somebody else's job. "I work for the City" is how the other garbage men put it—a mealymouthed bunch, afraid to come right out and get down to cases. It turns my stomach, makes me ashamed of them and, worse, of myself. The hell with them. I don't work for the City. I work for myself. The City pays me. I collect garbage. It's not so bad as you'd think. I wear thick gloves. You get used to it. Resignation, it pays a living wage. Sometimes you even enjoy it. When you get old you don't enjoy it anymore. You just pull up your zipper and go the route. They're kicking the old guys out anyway these days—they get something cushier. It's a new plan. After all, you don't want to see somebody's grandfather scraping shit eight-to-five in the rain. It's altogether too saintly. It makes the other guys, the young ones like myself—it makes us . . . *you* know, uncomfortable. D'you know? A vale of tears. You've got to keep the chatter up, yes, or everybody's going out of their minds.

I know about it! A man can get used to anything. Man—I've got my ideas about Man, too. It's my right. I'm one myself. That's how I see it. So I've got my ideas. Nick—Nicholas, the driver, an old Jew—he calls me the *philosophe*. "Here comes Angelo the *philosophe*." And why not? It passes the time, keeps up the chatter, makes everybody laugh. I do my part. Everybody on the truck does his part—that's why we get along so well. It's a regular vaudeville show. I tell you, come to think of it, I really like my job. Yes! Why not? I like to see what the goddamn city would do without us! One week I'd give them, and they'd be floating in their own stink, choking on it, dying in the gutters—all the tin cans, the stale food, the bad stew, the rotten vegetables, the banana peels, the fumy rags, the whole shebang slopping over the rooftops, right over the Empire State. I tell you, it'd be humorous. Evacuation, that would be the only answer. So I do my part, and small thanks I get. The hell with them. I don't care. Nobody gets much thanks in this world— nobody. I've got no kicks. I'm a philosopher. I like to think about Man—d'you know?—the mystery behind the garbage.

But then . . . yes . . . the mystery . . . that's what's bothering me. And today, today it's a very particular mystery. I'll tell you about it, my private catastrophe, my own little beast in the jungle. It's a short story . . . like Life itself! Life's a short story, that's my idea of it. Nick . . . Nicholas, he likes that idea. He laughed when I told him and I could see in his face his bad heart kick out a couple of times. It hurts those old Jews to laugh, too much rich food.

The catastrophe is that last night my brother-in-law came over for a short visit—he don't like to stay long at the garbage man's apartment, you see—and he read my palm. None of that gypsy crap. The real thing, authentic. He's a scientist, Jules is. A physicist. Very smart. A nut about being reasonable. Everything in its place, that's Jules. I respect him for it, but I tell you, deep down he gets under my skin. First of all he was against his sister marrying me. A Jewish girl and an Italian garbage man . . . it set his hair on end. And then, when we went and took the holy vows in the church, it was too much, of course, and poor old Jules's hair, every last thread, fell out the next day. At least it seemed so—he got bald right quick.

Jules doesn't believe in this palm-reading business. "I read a book last night," he tells me. Then he smiles, that little half-lip smile of his. "I'll give you a reading according to the master," he says. "An early death, a catastrophe. I give you two years, and that's it." Then he laughs. "So there's your palmistry for you, Angelo. It's all according to the book." He laughs again. He doesn't see my heart beating eight thousand miles a minute.

"Level with me, Jules," I say. "You really mean that's what the book says?"

"Your head line's broken under the Mount of Saturn," he says. "It's a classic sign. According to the book, Angelo, it's a sure thing. No hope. How's the job?"

How's the job! I don't sleep the rest of the night. I toss, I turn. All night I walk around. I want to *run* around, you see, I want to scream, punch a little on the walls, I'm tearing my hair. But I'm on my tiptoes, so as not to wake the kids and the neighbors, and I'm all of a hurricane in my guts. And the wife? She's sleeping too, like a baby. She doesn't take this thing seriously either. She's like her brother, reasonable, thank God. She's good for me, I have to admit. Keeps me on the straight and narrow, something solid in her to hold me to the earth when I run amok in my head. I'd be a madman on the moon by now if it weren't for her, my pretty Jew with the dark eyes. They could build a whole new Palestine around that woman—so sweet and reasonable and passionate, and righteous in her heart—and terrifying too she is, like the Holy Mother, because of her goodness. I think she knows the state I'm in, but doesn't want to let on. I bet she's just pretending to be asleep. I bet she's praying in her heart, that righteous perfect woman—not like her brother at all! In most respects.

Just before dawn I crawl back into bed so that I don't have to answer any questions. Maybe she was asleep after all. I don't know. It's a thing I've got to work out myself—man and God. That's how Life is sometimes . . . a short story . . . yes . . . and in my case, it looks, according to Jules's book, just a wee bit too short for my taste. I don't know. We'll find out.

I leave early for the station and sit in the truck and wait for the rest of the gang to show. I sit a long time. I stare out the windshield. All bright and clear it is this time of day. Really, garbage trucks are just about the cleanest things you ever did see . . . this time of day. There's some fellows come in at night to do the honors with soap and water. People don't know, don't appreciate. You'd think it was something disgraceful sometimes the way they talk, some people. We don't *make* the garbage, you know. It's them that make it. We just collect it. They are the ones that ought to be ashamed. But it doesn't work that way, as far as they can see. People don't look into things deeply enough.

Here comes Nicholas. He's early. I don't think he sleeps much, the poor old lecher, and his breath always stinks with wine in the morning, that sweet thick wine the Jews like. I see him now, in the distance, bent up forward, limping ever so slight, down through the rows and rows of trucks—there must be a million of them—tremendous and shining. They reek of yellow soap and yesterday's garbage—of a million yesterdays! —but of soap, too . . . that's the thing you notice, the soap. It's a strong smell that makes you proud and takes the edge off slightly of this degrading business. You get to thinking it *is* the Department of Sanitation, after all, no matter what people think. Garbage men indeed! The thing that gets your back up is all the scum on Welfare who look down their noses at you—a rotten useless pack of parasites, sucking up the taxpayer's blood money and making no less garbage than Governor Rockefeller himself, and then thumbing their noses at you because you're cleaning up their muck and stink and getting a pittance into the bargain. There's no justice in this world! No justice!

"Look! It's the *philosophe*," says Nicholas. He climbs up into the cab beside me. "You're here early, Angelo. What's wrong? Fighting with the Jews again?"

"I don't fight with my wife," I say. He has an odd sense of humor, Nicholas does.

"Ah, be careful. The Jews are no good, Angelo. A vicious crew. Mad as hatters, the whole lot."

He smiles and rubs his eyes. Then he squints and blinks as if something hurts him and he looks out over the herd of trucks.

"How is it, my son," he says, "that you are such a wonderful talker?"

My son! It gives me a good feeling.

"I guess it comes natural," I say. "Hey, you really think I'm a wonderful talker, Nicholas?"

"No," he says. "I am drunk. You are a stinking talker. I am confused. I listen to the voice in my head. And I say, 'Who is that talking?' I look about me. You are the only one here. Therefore, it must be Angelo. But it is not Angelo. It is the voice in my head. It is I, myself, Nicholas, that am the wonderful talker. Angelo, you are a stinking talker. You should go to night school, improve your mind. It is not right that a man throw away all his hours taking up garbage and sitting like a zombie in front of the television. You have resigned yourself to perdition."

"What about yourself?"

"Yes, I, too!" And he spits out the window.

The day is not lucky. I can smell it in the air. The rest of the gang arrives and pretty soon motors are roaring all over the yard and the fumes from the exhaust pipes, primeval and creepy, rise up over the hood. And then we're out.

I stand on the running board, the wind blows my hair. The gang's laughing, and Nicholas, he's driving like a demon. He even runs a couple of lights along the way, which isn't really like him at all. Altogether it's very strange and I can't help but snatch a look at my palm every now and then, to see if maybe my head line hasn't begun to grow together just a wee bit.

We're shooting down Thirteenth Street. Thirteen! It's everything bad signs today. There's not a good sign in the air. Signs—I've always been one for signs. Everything, every single last thing is a sign. That's my idea about it. The wife calls it superstition, Jules calls it neurosis. They get a word in their eye and then they can't see you for it, and that's how it is, I don't care.

Thirteenth Street. It's narrow. Just down in front of the unemployment bureau there's a car double-parked on the right. We're bearing down on it—and Nicholas, he ain't putting on the brakes. In fact, he steps on it a little. On our left is a hearse. He's neck and neck with us all the way. He steps on the gas too so as not to give us a chance to make it through the space. The both of them, Nicholas and the maniac in the black job on my left, are out of their skulls and all I can do is hold on and pray and there's my broken head line under the Mount of Saturn. Then just as we get to the space, Nick swerves it slightly to the left; the hearse, he swerves slightly to the right—like we're going to kiss hoods. But the film stops, the brakes are on, and there we are, the truck and the hearse with their noses in the space, at a deadlock, and nobody's backing out. Everybody wants through but there's room for only one at a time. No problem. Half an inch of courtesy clears the runway. One of them has got to back out.

"Back up a bit, Nick," I say.

Nick grits his teeth, shuts his eyes, and puts the side of his fist on the horn. The gang sets up a ruckus.

"Back up, you damn fool!" says Olson. He means the hearse, of course. The whole gang yells at the hearse; natch, we stick together. But me, I can't. I've never been much for screaming in the streets. I jump off the running board and walk around the hearse to the driver's side.

"Say, you better back up," I say. "Our man's in a stink. He'll sit there till the sky falls in."

"I have the right-of-way," says the driver. He's a young fellow, a boy almost, white fuzz on his cheek, and rosy as Cupid himself. He looks straight ahead at the black bill of his cap which is pulled way down over his eyes.

"Don't be a jackass," I say. "What difference does it make? Back up a little, let the old man through."

He just sits.

"What do you say?"

"I have the right-of-way," he says. His Adam's apple quivers, his ears are blushing at the lobes, and straightway I know he's not right completely in the head. I've got a nose for kooks. The kid's out of it. It's the job that did it to him probably. Driving a hearse at his age . . . there ought to be a law. I bet he don't know if he's coming or going.

"Be a sport," I say. "It's the old man . . . *you* know, he's older than you, he's seen a lot of hard times, he gets in moods like this."

Meanwhile the gang is raising Cain and shaking their fists, like the pirates in the movies do, hanging off the yardarms and making asses of themselves when the booty, the fancy dans, and the ladies sail by broadside. Nicholas sits in a heap and keeps his fist on the horn. I have to shout so as the driver can hear me. Hear . . . that's a laugh. The boy's deaf as a doornail. "I've got the right-of-way," and he clicks off. The right-of-way! Did you ever? A crowd's gathering. They're eating it up. There's a show in the streets, fellas! Look at the garbage truck! Look at the hearse! Boy oh boy! It gives your stomach a turn, I can tell you.

"Move out!" I scream. "The whole block's in an uproar! The cops will be down on us in a shake, you'll see!"

"I have the right-of-way."

"Screw your goddamn right-of-way! What's the difference whose right-of-way it is when the old man's sitting on his horn and busting everybody's eardrums? D'you like crowds or something? That's it! You . . ."

"I've got the right-of-way."

I see the cops shuffling around the corner and coming down toward us. This will be bad for Nicholas. Why, I bet he could lose his job for this. They'll put him back on the truck again, scraping cans like me. That's not good. It's a terrible mess.

"I tell you what: here's a fin, kid. Swallow your pride and right-of-way just this one time—what do you say?"

I put a five-dollar bill under his nose, kind of tickle his nether lip. I've been around.

"I've got the right-of-way," he says, just with his lips, in a whisper that cuts the noise and blows the bill, ever so slight, like a wind in the leaves.

"Sure, Jack. You've got the biggest right-of-way in town and everybody's scared to death of you! But, you see, the cops are coming, Nicholas is going to get canned, and the horn . . . the horn's going to bust our ears wide open!"

He yawns, it's a great big yap he's got, and he bites the bill out of my hand and sucks it into his maws. He chews. I can hear his choppers going a mile a minute in there, then he puckers up as if he's going to whistle a pretty tune, and blows the bits and pieces of two hours' reward out the window in a fine stream. It catches the wind and dances away uptown like a swarm of green flies. The horn stops blowing. The crowd quiets down and looks up. The silence is so terrible that you'd think it was the Holy Ghost or something up there instead of just a lousy five bucks. The two cops inspect the front of the hoods and rub their chins. Nicholas appears at my side. He sticks his head in the window and whispers in the driver's ear.

"The day is passing," he says. "Let us not bicker, my friend. The garbage and the corpses await us. We must preserve the order, maintain the balance . . . eh?"

"I have the right-of-way," says the driver.

Nicholas pulls away, his eyes bulge.

"That is so!" he says. "He speaks the truth, Angelo!" Nick puts his head in the window again. "I concede," he says. "I acknowledge your priority and am willing to allow you to pass before me through the space. The situation, however, is complicated by the bumpers. Your bumper is directly behind mine— do you see? I am willing to retreat, but, in order for me to do so, it will be necessary for you to retreat a few inches first. Then shall I be able to pull backward and allow you to go your way. It is quite simple and requires merely that you compromise a few inches."

Nicholas has a fine style, a silver tongue, but the driver's not moved. Kids are hard, cold.

"I have the right-of-way," he says, and I tell you it's just about the last time I can put up with that remark. Nicholas is calm.

"Surely, that's clear. You have both the right and the way. And I, Nicholas, have nothing but a garbage truck and a chauffeur's license. Nevertheless, the traffic is piling up behind us. What shall we do? I am at your service and attend whatever reasonable suggestion you might offer."

He was right. The cars were lined up for three blocks behind us, the horns had begun to blow all over the place, they were trapped, there was no out, no place to turn. A few of the drivers were screaming out their windows and waving their arms like the puppets in the park. I can't restrain myself any longer.

"Did you see what this bastard did with my money, Nick? He's a lunatic! He ought to be locked up!"

"Locked up is right!" That's one of the cops. They've snuck up behind us.

"We're going to lock the whole bunch of you up," says the other, "if you don't clear out."

"Nicholas here is perfectly willing to back up, officer," I say. "It's this lunkhead that's the stubborn one."

The officer, the tall one, looks at me. He looks at Nicholas. The eye of justice. I smile. I mainly like cops. They have a tough job.

"Come on out of the car, son," he says.

"I have the right-of-way," says the kid.

Did you ever? I've seen all kinds of audacity now. The kid's got some guts, you have to give him that.

"Is the back empty?" says the officer.

He means is there a corpse in the back.

The boy for the first time turns his head and looks at us.

"It is always empty," he says.

That's a wacky thing to say. Nicholas, he starts in to weeping and it's altogether too lively and fancy for my taste. Oh, but I know what he's talking about all right.

The next thing I know Nicholas is back up in the cab of the truck, the motor's revving, and the truck is smashing the hearse . . . first little bumps—we, the cops, the kid, and myself, hurry up out of the way—and then big bumps and crashes. The rest of the gang's jumped off the track and Nicholas is jerking the machine back and forth against one of the hearse's fenders. But he can't maneuver much in that small space and the

fender is the only thing he can get at. He's also mashing hell out
of the car that's double-parked on the right, and that's the one
that's getting the worst of it. "The innocent always get the brunt
of the madness in this world," whispers the kid in my ear. I don't
answer and he walks away from me. The cops have their pistols
out of their holsters. They're shouting something or other at
Nicholas but I'll be damned if I can make out what they're saying amid the general racket, the metal smashing, the horns, the
put-out puppets yakking it up back there. It's all in the hand. I'd
like to have got Jules to read Nicholas' palm . . . the cops'
palms, too, and the kid's—everybody's! Then we'd have been
able to figure things out, to sit down, look over the lines on the
map, and reason with one another.

"Let's be reasonable!" Who said that? I must have imagined
it. Voices like that happen to me sometimes. It's either some
kind of feedback I get from the educational channel or it's my
brother-in-law. I hear Jules in my head a lot.

The unemployment bureau's emptied out. The jobless stand
on the curb, lapping it up—a free show. They pour down the
steps and out the door to the street. Dapper as everybody else
they are. They ought to wear badges so you can tell them apart
from the rest of us. They pour out two by two through the
double doors. Jules is among them . . . Jules! He comes out
of the unemployment bureau. Maybe he was doing scientific
research up there. I run across the street to him. He takes me by
the elbow and stares out at the truck bashing away.

"Angelo," he says. "I've quit my job. I've decided to devote
myself entirely to the study of palmistry."

"Jules! You gave up physics!"

"I am a palmist," he says. "I have given up nothing."

"You don't believe in that crap! Palmistry! That's for
gypsies!"

He smiles, takes off his hat, and turns the other side of his face to me. He's got a golden ring in his right ear! It glitters like neon and sequins. It hurts my eyes.

"What about the wife and the kids? They need you, Jules. And the university needs you, too! Think what a bad name it's going to give the school when they find out you've chucked physics and run off with a ring in your ear!"

"I shall continue to pursue my studies, Angelo. Physics has a very special place in my heart. Only now my whole heart is in the grip of palmistry. Everything has changed!"

"You've gone off your rocker!"

"Mere psychology," he says. "And, frankly, Angelo, that discipline has always bored me. Off my rocker? That simply has no meaning for me. I am atomic. I am photon. I am flesh. I have lines in my hand. I am entitled to the benefits of unemployment insurance."

I don't know what to do, to say! Everything's topsy-turvy. I run to the truck and leap onto the running board.

"Stop it!" I cry. "Nicholas! Get a grip on yourself!"

But he can't hear me for the havoc. A pistol shot gives us a start for a minute, Nick and me, but then he's at it again. It's the cops. They're shooting out the tires, the damn fools, and Nicholas goes on, riding on the rims now. Shooting out the tires has got them naught but a rise in the clatter. The metal rolls roughshod over the asphalt. More cops have arrived. The whole force it looks like.

"You're not a real Jew, Nicholas!" I shout in his ear. "You're an impostor! There's never been a Jew in the whole lousy history of the world with a name like Nicholas! Own up! You're a wop like me! Or a Greek. That's it! Nick, the Greek! Ha, ha!"

He stops. It worked. He looks at me and starts bawling. He puts his face in his arms and falls forward on the horn in the middle of the steering wheel. It sets up an awful wail. The cops come around to us. Now that it's all over they want to show how brave they are.

"Back!" I announce. I'm standing on the running board like on a pedestal above them. They look up and stop, believe it or not. I think the confusion's got them down.

Jules walks through the crowd and inspects palms. Slowly, methodically, he tells fortunes, and one by one the faces go pale and green along the sidewalk. Jules seems not to care about the truck, or Nicholas, or the cops. He is patient and reasonable— he hasn't changed a bit! Only the mob changes. The cops bicker, Nicholas bawls, the horn blows, but one by one they leave, the people. They wander off down the street looking at their palms. They're mad to find the mystery, they're checking out the lines, each one his own. Soon there's no one on the sidewalk and Jules walks down the three-block row of cars and predicts for all the passengers. The cars are abandoned. Nobody looks at one another, nobody cares for anything except the lines in their hands. Glassy-eyed and loose, like the addicts up in Harlem, the people shamble down the street, and nobody cares that the hearse has got the garbage truck by the bumper. I can feel the head line on my hand grow together, together. The break beneath the Mount of Saturn has disappeared. The line runs along as merry as the Hudson River with no monkey business.

"Nick!" I cry. "My head line's grown together! D'you hear?"

But Nicholas don't care. He keeps weeping on the horn. Why does Nicholas weep?

Jules comes around and reads the cops' palms, and they go away too, one by one, like everybody else. After all, they're human beings too.

"Jules, I'm thinking you ought to read Nick's palm, too."

"He's read his own," says Jules. "That's why he's in such a state."

"Is it that bad then, Jules? His palm?"

"Every single palm on this planet is bad, Angelo. Do you see the people wandering away looking at their hands? I lied to every one of them."

"What kind of a lie is it that you told them to put them out like that?"

"I read their palms—that was the lie."

"You mean it's a fraud?"

"By reading their palms I conned them into the fiction that each one of them is bound up with the mystery, but they're not bound, Angelo, and they've got about as much to do with the mystery as your garbage there has to do with the incinerator and that's about it."

"And what about you, Jules?"

"I," says he, grabbing me by the shoulders, "am immortal, you dumb wop!"

He sticks his palm in front of my face. I see that his lifeline is a perfect circle.

"That signifies eternal life, Angelo!"

Then he turns around and snaps his fingers.

"Driver!" he calls, and the kid that drives the hearse comes running. That Jules, he's got a commanding personality. Snaps his fingers and everybody jumps.

"Where to?" says the kid.

Jules just smiles. The kid smiles back. Then they bust out laughing and the kid opens the back door of the hearse, stands aside, bows as Jules steps in, and poof, gone, vanished behind the black curtain, just like that . . . my brother-in-law! The kid slips in behind the wheel, shifts into reverse, then into first, swings around the side of the truck, and they're off. I'm alone with Nicholas and he won't stop bawling for love nor money.

"Nick! The space is clear! The hearse is gone! Let's get going!"

I open the door and a heap of garbage that's piled up on the seat behind the steering wheel comes tumbling down on me. I'm flabbergasted with stink and filth, and Nicholas ain't there no more. A pretty black-and-white alley cat crawls out from under some tin cans that have fallen at my feet, and runs away down the street. I'd like to go after it and curl up in a nice dark alley somewhere, just the two of us, and think things over. But who's going to clean up the mess? Jules has made zombies of the rest of the gang, Nicholas has turned into garbage, the kitten's run off, and now there's nobody left but me to tidy up. My head line's broke again, just like that. I felt it snap. But that doesn't make any difference. The hearse has got out of the way and there's nothing to prevent the truck from moving out. Looks like I've got to be everything today—driver, garbage collector, foreman—at least till tomorrow when they send some replacements. There's always replacements ready, a whole line of poor slobs just dying to get a job with the city.

Poor Jules! D'you know, I'm kind of glad he let me in on the hoax. I feel much better about it now. Still there's something to it, no matter what Jules says. Something in the palm. One thing I don't get is how come Jules drove off in the hearse if he's as immortal as he says he is. I mean, where did the hearse take him? I know he's not going to wind up in the city dump like Nicholas. Jules is going someplace special. Not like the rest of us. But where? Where's Jules going and how does he rate? How come his lifeline makes a circle and nobody else's does? Maybe he carved it in there with a penknife himself, just to show off.

I make it through the day somehow. It's a big job for one man alone, and when I get home everything's just as it always is, as if nothing in the world had happened. I don't say a word at dinner and afterward I go to bed. I wake up in the middle of the night. There's a noise beside me in the bed. The kid, the driver of the hearse, with his black hat on lies on my wife. He's got a wide black cape wrapped around the two of them and his mouth is clamped over hers, as if he wanted to take the breath out of her. And she lies in his arms, as if she knew it wasn't any use to kick up a fuss and that the one good thing she might accomplish tonight would be to keep peace in the dark so as to protect me from the sight of him. I turn away and don't let on I know, and put my face in my hand. The tears run down the gulley of my palm, the lifeline. There's a stir beside me. I don't turn. She blows in my ear. It's warm and soothes me . . . no, wait, it's not the wife. It's the kid who blows in my ear, but I don't turn to look. I know who it is. I know the sound of her breath and that is not her breath.

Dawn is breaking. The stink of garbage rises ever so slowly, like the sun, and you can hear the supers rolling the cans on the sidewalk. Today, in every heap that's thrown into the truck, I will look for you . . . Nicholas.

The Horse's Ass

I am on the road—do you see?—the old rock-ridden road from
the marketplace to my home. This was several years ago. I am
sitting on my cart and watching the bright gray spot on the
horizon, just there where the sun was a minute ago. I am
dreamy, tired, and smiling, because I have had a profitable day
and have sold the five buckets of wild berries that my children
gathered the day before, the bright red and green tapestry
woven by my patient wife, and also the thin little booklet of
poems by the great master of our district, which I have copied
on fine linen in a most splendid and extravagant script and
bound in the rich leather tanned by my eldest son. There is a
chill in the air. I turn up my collar and hold my elbows close
into my ribs. Wisps of steam rise out of my horse's mouth. He
plods along slowly, my horse. He is a sullen wrathful creature,
and whimsical. He has no name. He is simply the horse. At first
it had never occurred to us that he must have a name, until
people began to inquire, "What's the old boy's name?" Name?
Why, he has no name. He is our horse. We have but one. If we
had two, then there would be some sense in naming them, so as
to distinguish between them. As it is, the horse suffices, and
there is no confusion. Oh, certainly we call him other things—

all manner of things, in fact, depending upon our mood at the moment. But these are not in truth names anymore than my youngest daughter's name is "pretty one" or "little devil." No, properly speaking, he is just the horse.

It had begun in innocence, the namelessness of our horse, and we never gave it a thought, until people began to make it a source of conversation and of good-natured jokes. "That's very sensible," they would say, or they would come up and give the horse a lump of sugar and say, "Hello, horse!" and then go off into peals of laughter. And I would laugh with them. And it has had some influence, a lasting influence, if I may say so. Why, just the other day I overheard a farmer in conversation with a peddler. "The mule? Why, the mule has no name. He is our mule. We have but one. If we had two, then . . ." And so on. So now it has become a source of pride to us. I feel happy and it flatters my vanity that I have had some influence of some kind in this world.

So, I was riding along, in the twilight, you see, and it was a Friday, I remember, and I was thinking . . . what was I thinking about at the time? Of course. I was thinking about Saturday. I was thinking about the cool waters. Every Saturday we go there. The children go bathing, or, when it is too cold, they sit with my wife and myself under the immense trees, on a blanket spread on the grass, and we talk and look at the rippling stream that runs on and on, for miles and miles, down and around the slopes and valleys, and into the big river that empties into the sea. We never miss a Saturday, even in the winter. For then the water freezes and there is skating and we hitch the horse to the great sled with the red runners and glide across the snow. It is very pleasant. Sometimes it rains, and then we put a large cover over the cart and a canvas over the horse's back and we ride out in the rain. People laugh at that. I do not blame them, and there is something to it, their laughter. I see that. But what can I do?

It has become a custom, and I like to see the water falling into the stream. I like to hear the thunder and see the lightning while I sit with my family, snug and dry in the cart. Saturday is a good day to think about, for me. That is how I remember, even now, what I was thinking about at that moment in the twilight. I remember because I was always thinking about Saturday in those times. Whenever I was alone, I thought about the cool waters, and the cart . . .

But then—do you see?—suddenly my horse stops in the middle of the road. He swings his head around and looks at me and then walks off to the shoulder and stops by a small thick evergreen, and no matter how hard I tug at the reins, no matter how hard I whip him or how harshly I shout, he will not return to the road. He simply stands by the bush and plunges his head in among the pungent leaves. I step down from the cart to see what I can do.

"Come along!" I say and give a good tug at the bit. But he is resolved and stubborn. He does not budge. There is nothing to be done, for I have acquired neither the cruelty, nor the detachment, nor the bestial intuition, that are so necessary if one is to be masterful with animals. That is my nature. In situations of this sort, I have always resorted to mere patience, of which I have a sufficient measure, and that has always seen me through, patience.

I turn my back on the horse and fold my arms across my chest and wait. The sky darkens. Some hours—I know not how many—pass. It is a clear night with a full moon and there is a warm breeze every now and then out of the east. Something stirs behind me. I turn around, not immediately though, but after a few moments—so as to show that I am not overanxious —and there, facing me, is the horse. He looks directly into my eyes and stands very straight and proud beside the evergreen, which glows now, almost golden in the moonlight, like the shimmering colors of the dye my wife uses on her tapestries. I say nothing, nor do I make any movement. "Tomorrow you shall go to the waters," says the horse, "but you shall walk. And every Saturday hereafter you shall go to the waters, and always you shall walk, and I shall not go with you." And then he turns from me and ambles out to the road and waits for me to climb into the cart, and we continue homeward.

I speak little when I arrive. I say nothing of the incident by the evergreen, but retire directly after supper. I remember muttering, however, as my wife was clearing the table, "That's a lazy beast, that horse of ours. He thinks of nothing but his own comfort." My wife looks at me, quizzically, but I say nothing more and go to bed. I do not sleep that night, for I am plagued with visions of the horse.

The next morning, Saturday, I rise early. My wife and children are already at the breakfast table and eager to set forth to the waters. I hear the stomping outside the barn, which means my eldest son is there, hitching the horse to the cart. I eat breakfast and we go outdoors. My eldest son is up in the driver's seat, smiling. The horse is sullen and hangs his head as I approach.

"Come down," I say to my son. "Unhitch the horse. We are walking today."

Walking! Everyone is amazed.

"It is nice weather," I say. "The sun is out, it is brisk. The walk will do us good."

They will not hear of it. They imagine I am joking or merely being foolish, and all, except myself, prepare to climb into the cart. I wait for them to take their seats, and then, looking up at them, I tell of yesterday's incident. No one answers me when I have done, but they fall to whispering among themselves and stealing suspicious questioning glances at me from time to time. At last they come down with a forced air of gaiety, and my son unhitches the horse. It is a bright clear day, and, just as I predicted, the walk does us good.

"Perhaps," says my son about midway in the journey, "—perhaps we ought to buy an automobile."

"What for?" I ask.

"Why, for Saturdays!" he cries.

"We must walk on Saturdays," I tell him. "Were you not listening?"

"That's not what the horse meant, Papa," he says, laughing. I detect a note of condescension in his voice. I have heard that tone before, when he talks to his youngest sister. I do not like it.

Every Saturday thereafter, for the rest of the year, we walk. As luck would have it, all the Saturdays have clear weather. Even in the winter, the weather is not hostile to our journey. Though there is snow on the ground, there is no snow in the air on Saturdays. It does not fall on this day, as though all the blizzards had lain down in the barn with the horse, to rest. This pleases us, and, truly, we are all of us the more healthy for the exercise that year. There is a flush in our cheeks and the children have grown supple and lean. My eldest son continues to plague me with his automobiles, but I am firm on the subject.

At the end of the year, on the very anniversary of the evergreen incident, in fact, the horse dies. The next day, Saturday, as we are walking, as is our habit, to the waters, I notice that my eldest son is particularly thoughtful and preoccupied. He speaks little, and, for the first time in a year, does not once for the entire day mention automobiles. One would imagine he were grieving over the death of the horse, but I have other notions.

On Sunday we have a family conference at the breakfast table. What to do for transportation? All of them are in favor of buying an automobile. A secondhand automobile, they say, will be less expensive than a good horse, and it will be quicker, more efficient, and it will last longer. My eldest son, however, does not speak. He takes no sides and excuses himself from the table as soon as he can. No decision is reached. In the evening he returns driving an automobile. We must of course run outdoors to greet him and everyone is disproportionately amazed.

"I found it on the road!" he cries. The muscles in his face are quivering, his eyes dance nervously. There is something altogether strange and unnatural in his behavior, and though it seems he is trying to avoid my eyes, his glance is irresistibly drawn to mine at every other word.

"It's as if it dropped right down from heaven!" he babbles. "It's as if the old horse had left it in his place. We ought to be grateful. And . . . and humble!"

All are eager to agree with him. And even I do not venture to contradict. After all, what might I say? Shall I call my son a liar? Shall I call him foolish and deceived? He too claims to have had a revelation. I am obliged, though loath, to accept it.

I learn to drive. I learn quickly, and, frankly, I enjoy it. They were right. It is more efficient. But on Saturdays we walk.

"But it's so foolish!" cries my son. "The horse is dead. It's clear, absolutely *clear,* that he meant only that we should walk to give him a day of rest. Why are you so stubborn? What good is our walking now? To give a machine a rest? Machines have no feelings! Papa! It's so foolish!"

"And who said," I answer, "that we walk to give the horse a rest? Who said that!"

"You did!"

"I never said such a thing. I said that we walk because it was said by the horse that we should. And if the horse rises again and tells me that we should ride, then we shall ride. I do not need your interpretations, my son. I do not myself venture interpretations, so how should I honor yours? Have you heard the voice that I have heard? I have witnessed a single action which confounds, and you would have me submit it to a logic principled upon comfort?"

But it is no good. Years have passed since then. It seems that

I have been proved wrong. I make no sense. The automobile improves but the weather grows bad. It rains every Saturday, as if in spite. A stench rises from the bed of the stream. The children do not swim anymore. Nor do they skate. The ice cracks at the slightest provocation. But still one walks, one goes to the waters.

I stand before my house with my son at my side. There is a light rain. The automobile opens its hood and says, "You may ride on Saturdays. There is no need to walk."

My son looks at me and smiles triumphantly.

"Indeed . . ." I say, and peer suspiciously into the motor. The hood clamps shut, nearly severing my nose from my face. One has come upon a rude age.

"A miracle, Papa!" cries my son. He jumps up and down ecstatically. I daresay he is transfigured.

"Of which miracle, my son, are you speaking?" I say.

"This one . . . the automobile! It spoke!"

"And that is a miracle, eh?"

"As much as the horse was!"

"Indeed!"

"Indeed what?" he says, narrowly. He is troubled.

"There can be but one miracle," I say. "And that is the first. After the first miracle, what seems to be a miracle is no longer miraculous. As soon as it repeats itself, it enters the realm of predictability, and the predictable is not miraculous. There is a bit of philosophy for you, my son. No, leave me in peace. I have had my miracle. Don't spoil it for me."

He runs away. He has become quite insane from this novelty of a talking automobile. But I do not worry. He runs off into the woods, but he has a good head and will return, both home and to his senses. Patience.

He comes back dragging the horse. Just as I had expected he has gone to its grave and dug it up. The beast has remained remarkably intact and there is not the slightest trace of decomposition. My son weeps, sweats, and he is breathless with the exertion; he throws himself like a pagan on his knees and begins to apostrophize womanishly.

"Rise, O horse!" he cries. "Speak! The word! The word! Save us from my father's everlasting philosophy! From his stubbornness!"

The horse gathers itself together and stands on all fours.

"You may ride on Saturdays," it says and lies down dead once again.

My son, still on his knees, crawls toward me, and clutches my legs.

"Papa!" he cries. "The horse! It speaks! You promised!"

"I promised?"

"If the horse rises again, you said, and tells me to ride, then we shall ride."

"Did I say that?"

"Indeed you did!"

"Then I was a fool when I said it. One is but mortal and cannot forever be master of one's tongue. One slips betimes. Forgive me. Your father was a fool."

"But the horse commanded you! You heard! With your own ears!"

"Ah yes, with these imperfect flowers. Indeed I did! . . . But tell me: you realize naturally that the horse in this miraculous career of his thus far has commanded me twice. Once on the road and once just now before the house. Now, of which command are you speaking? Of the first or of the second?"

"Of the second! The one just now! Of course!"

"Good. And why should I obey the second and not the first?"

"Oh no you don't . . ." he says, soberly, of a sudden, and he stands up and looks at me out the corner of his eye. "I know what you're going to say so you might as well save it."

"And what was I going to say?"

"That . . ."

"I was going to say nothing. I was merely asking your opinion. Now which will it be? The first or the second?"

"The second."

"No. The first. You see, my son? You make a very poor prophet."

He is exasperated, and thus, to give him a useful project upon which to focus his anguish, I assign him the task of dragging the horse back to its grave. He returns in the evening exhausted and morose, but calm. He does not speak to me once the remainder of the week. On Saturday morning we set forth for the waters. I open the front door and I start down the steps. At the last moment—but it is too late, of course, by then—I see his foot stuck out in front of my ankles. I trip, I fall, I am in pain on the ground. I have broken my legs.

The doctor is sent for from the village, a kindly man.

"No more walking for you, I'm afraid. The bones are smashed beyond repair—and then you are not so young anymore. But have heart. The pain will subside."

The pain will subside. Indeed. The automobile, my son, the doctor, and the horse itself have told me to ride . . . each in his own way. Why is everyone so very interested in my riding? We do not go to the waters this day of course and for two weeks I stay at home. I do not go to market. How should I go? I convalesce. I meditate. But I miss the waters. It has been two weeks now. One feels unclean after so long a drought and longs for the sound of the rapids. Melancholy soothes me. The doctor was right. The pain in my legs subsides, but it wells up again in unexpected places. All of my life I have been shuffling a very pretty little pain from one part of me to another. We have become greatly attached, this pain and I, and I should find it hard to go on without it—just as I find it hard to go on without the waters. But then there is the walking. What shall we do about the walking?

I summon my son to my bedside. It is Saturday. I feel fresh, eager.

"We shall go to the waters today. Lift me up."

He looks at me in wonder, but I shut my eyes and assume an attitude of resignation.

He cradles me, as though I were a child or a bride, one arm under my knees and the other around my back, and takes me outdoors. The family follows, officiously whispering in the rear.

He steers toward the automobile.

"No, my son. We shall walk."

His face turns red, his eyes bulge, he is incredulous. One would have thought from the look in his eyes that he had seen . . . a ghost . . . as they say. He says nothing. A true testament of awe. No womanish ecstasy here. I think that for the first time in his life he has been truly confounded. He takes to the road. My wife is weeping softly behind us and nodding with dissatisfaction, but she dares not dispute with me. The younger children are merry, laughing at the strange figure we cut, my son and I. My son is wonderfully stoic and rather handsome with the skin taut on his face and neck, the fury blooming in his cheeks. I attempt to engage him in conversation, to divert him.

"And what is more logical," I begin, "than that I should use your legs for the journey? Are not your legs indeed my legs? Are you not of my seed? Is the father not the son? And the son the father? Are we not at last one and the very same? And does this not fulfill the first commandment, then, of the horse—both in the spirit and the very letter? And is it not fine that you should carry me, just as I carried you when you were a babe? And does not the thought of this fill your lungs with blitheness and rejuvenate your weary arms?"

At which point he veers to the shoulder of the road and drops me into the ditch. One is amazed, aware suddenly of all the ligaments and joints in one's body. Hitherto unknown pains rush in from all points of the globe. There is a deal of shrieking and moaning from my wife and children. My son has run off—he is gone. I have not seen him since. The doctor appears. He smiles. I recover. Ever the same cycle. Misfortune and fortune. Yet one does not let go of it, this life. I have hired a gymnast. He has taught me to walk on my hands. And therefore, in this way, on Saturday I amuse the children, and go to the waters in fine and faithful style. My wife, good woman, grows careworn and dry as dust. It abuses her sense of propriety to travel thus beside the inverted man. One sympathizes with her. I did cut such a fine upright figure on our wedding day and now she is chained to a senile circus performer who gasps and sputters for miles and miles without let.

But my arms, you see, my arms grow strong in my old age. Yes, yes, very strong . . .

What of It?

It was a dark, a sleepy night in the nuthouse. The radiators were blasting away—banging, clanging . . . I dreamed of trains. I was asleep. My job was to stay awake. But it was stuffy. The steam that bubbled in the pipes was absolute morphine. We were all asleep, all us watchmen. There were five of us and a hundred inmates. The inmates were kids—gangsters, loonies . . . a sordid bunch. I didn't have to bother much with 'em, they'd be asleep when I arrived and not quite awake when I'd leave. A cushy job. Herding nightmares. You could handle it lying down, with your blinkers shut, and we all did. Paid sleep. Oh there was a clock to punch all right, every two hours, but we never bothered much about it, nobody ever checked the tape so it was all the same. Sometimes just for the sake of form one of us would make the rounds. But that didn't happen too often. After all, our sleep was being paid for—precious stuff—we didn't want to waste too much of it. And this particular night, like I say, it was heavy, nobody was wasting nothing.

About seven that morning, a half hour before the day shift was supposed to arrive and wake the kiddies, I get a hell of a jolt. It's Kleeger . . . the watchman from next door, a champion snoozer, ten spotless years with the firm, a career unblemished by even the merest speck of industry. He's shaking me. I give him one disinterested eye. I'm horizontally annoyed.

"Knock off, Kleeg—"

He grabs my hair. "Scherfel," says he, "Scherf—they're gone. Gone!"

"Cool it," I tell him and give him the broad expanse of both my lids. Then I'm asleep again, roaring down the track on the midnight special, the whole country's whizzing by . . . Chattanooga, Charleston, Cucamonga . . .

Bash, crash, clang-clang . . . derailed . . . a bloody mess . . . bodies fling out the window and pile upon the gravel . . . the train's burning, the whistle's screaming . . . glass all over the place . . . everyone's dead . . . not me though . . . I'm standing bolt upright, right up there, right smack on top of the heap . . . the watchman of the dead, that's me . . .

"That's me!" I'm screaming. Kleeger's got me by both lapels, he's holding me on my feet and shaking me.

"Scherfel! Scherf! Wake up, wake up!"

I give him one good rip-roaring nightmarish sock in the belly, delivering him promptly to the far corner of the room. He's not dazed, not angry, he sits there with the same earnest expression on his mug. "Scherfel," he says, "listen to me. They're gone! Gone! D'you understand?"

"Well then," says I, "good riddance to 'em . . . life's like that. Here one minute, gone the next. I swear, Kleeg, you're the most excitable individual I've ever met. Just stop and think a moment, relax, there's nothing to be excited about, nothing at all. They're gone . . . right? Well, so what! Is that a reason to be waking people out of their beds? They're gone . . . well, believe me, lots of good folks have gone in the past, are going this very minute and shall in the future be going even farther! Believe me! Even farther!"

He stands up, Old Kleeger does, and he takes me by the

elbow, very gently mind you, for he knows something about sleep, its effects and salutations. All the same his lips are tight as a prison and his teeth are scraping up a hell of a hullabaloo in there . . . I can hear 'em. I get a foggy presentiment . . .

He leads me into the bedroom and flicks on the light. The light has a curious effect. Kleeger's uncanny fact floods me, gluts my pores, spits in my eyes. My pupils wince. I'm aghast.

We rush out. I'm leading this time . . . I'm dragging Kleeger by the collar . . . it's all he can do to keep up . . . we race through the bedrooms, all ten of 'em—all the same . . . a morgue . . . the blankets stripped off and scattered on the floor . . . every bed empty, white as a sheet . . .

Kleeger and I, we wake the other three watchmen—Bleary, Fergus and Pinsk—we foregather on the stairwell.

"I knew it!" cries Pinsk. "I knew someday it'd come to this horrible pass! Awful! God's punished us at last for our heinous crimes! Gentlemen, let us pray. Let us bow our heads and ask forgiveness of the almighty! Let us on bended knees beg safe-keeping for our little urchins—wherever they may be. Gentlemen, the crisis hath tiptoed past us . . . and we have o'erslept it!"

I ram my hanky in his yap . . . there's no time . . . not a second to lose.

"Listen, gang," says I, "there's twenty-three minutes before the day shift shows. We gotta move fast. Kleeg, you scout the canyon. Bleary, the orchard. Fergus, the pines. Pinsk—sorry, old man—spit out the rag and hightail it for the athletic field."

"What about you, General?" says Kleeg.

I give 'em all the Metro Goldwyn Mayer pause, a twenty thousand dollar sigh. "I'll take the river."

Pinsk gasps: "The river . . . Godamercy, help us. . . ."

"But you've got thirteen minutes and that's it, then everybody back, that'll give us another ten to figure how we're gonna get ourselves out of this. I got a feeling . . . never mind . . . get going."

We bundle down the steps . . . all trepidation. Once out in the open the five of us fly in different directions. It's cold, none of us have coats—we sober up pretty quick . . .

I'm down at the river before I know it. It's rolling in, the fog I mean, thick, not a crack of sky in the whole caboodle. One solid gray puff . . . the river casts its shadow upside-down . . . a gray shadow . . . it slides off the surface . . . disengages . . .

I can't see a blasted thing—not my shoes, my hands, the river itself. I hear it sloshing around over there though . . . slosh-slosh . . . frightful—not another sound . . . brrr-creepy. . . .

"Anybody here?"

Anybody answers and I'll drop my load on the spot. I'm a blind man in a traffic jam. Nobody answers. Thank goodness.

I swim back through the fog. We all five show up at the same time.

"What do we do now?" says Kleeger.

"Pray," says Pinsk.

"Pray yer ass," says Fergus.

"Precisely my sentiments," says Bleary. He's been to college, Bleary has.

"I have a plan," says I and make it up as I go along. The day shift's on its way. I see the station wagon pulling away from the Staff Quarters up at the top of the hill. "When the day jerks get here, fellas, we just keep mum, see? 'Everything is okay, guys' . . . and all that shit. But we hold 'em outside a minute or two . . . we gab, we fumble around our pockets for the keys, anything . . . just keep 'em outside a couple extra minutes . . . make 'em late . . . get it?"

"What good's *that* gonna do?" says Kleeg. He's thick.

"You're thick, Kleeg," I tell him. "Listen, by the time the day counselors get into the rooms we'll be gone, get it? Gone. And it'll be a good ten minutes into the day shift before anything's reported. Then whose fault's it gonna be? Eh?"

"Ah, Mr. Scherfel," says Pinsk, "there's no doubt about fault. The fault is ours! Heaven help us—it's ours!"

There's nothing for it. I lay him out then and there. Kleeg slings him across his back in a fireman's carry. The station wagon pulls up and vomits its baggy-eyed crew. Looks as if the day boys have been up all night. We dump Pinsk across the back seat.

"Heart attack," I explain.

Everyone gasps. The driver wants to jet it to the hospital but I tell him to wait. Meanwhile we jaw around the wagon a bit, us nights and days. Pinsk provides a morbid topic. We could talk all day. It goes on fifteen minutes until I give the high sign and then Kleeger, Bleary, Fergus and I pile into the back seat on top of Pinsk who's beginning to show signs of life. I sit on his ear and hold his nose behind my back.

"Which hospital?" queries the driver.

"Hospital!" says I, incensed. "My dear man, don't you know that our Pinsk here is a Christian Scientist?"

"No shit . . ."

"Absolutely on the line."

"He looks Jewish to me."

"He converted."

"No shit . . ."

"Just last year. His wife was costing him a fortune in doctor bills—gall bladder—so he converted . . . converted her too . . . died the following week, she did."

"No shit . . ."

"Good old Pinsk . . . he made her a Christian none too soon—snatched her in the very nick from the maws of perdition. Drive on."

We arrive at the Staff Quarters. Pinsk is struggling. I give him a knock on the block, he's out cold. We drag him inside—we gather in my room. I tie Pinsk to a chair with clothesline and gag him firmly. We all sack out on the floor, even me—as a democratic gesture I forego the bed—in five minutes we're all fast asleep,—even Pinsk. . . . It's been a hard night's work.

I wake up at noon—everybody up!

"What now?"

"First," say I, "untie Pinsk and pull that rag out of his mouth." Kleeger does the honors, but Pinsk—he ain't movin'.

"He ain't movin'," says Fergus.

Bleary rushes over to feel the forehead—a big chance for Bleary. Bleary's flunked out of medical school when he was young and has spent the twenty years since then trying to prove to himself and everybody else that he would have made a great doctor—

He looks at us, he toys with the medallion slung around his neck like a stethoscope.

"Dead," says he—scientifically grave. "Stone cold."

"What now?"

"Flush him down the john."

We do. He goes down easy. He's thin as tissue paper. At last he's where he belongs. One can now shit upon Pinsk with a clear conscience and under the most sanitary conditions. Everybody does. Christian Scientists have a rough time in this world.

"Ring up the school, why dontcha . . ." says Fergus.

Good idea. I ring up.

"Hello, Penelope? This is Scherfel. How's yer face?"

She sighs. Penelope abuses herself all day under the typewriter. Everybody knows . . . nobody minds . . . her manuscripts are flawless, her speed is champion, she's stacked with efficiency and padded with courtesy . . . she likes her bit of oblivion like anyone else, after all.

"How's tricks at the school?"

"Fine," she says. "It's empty."

"Empty?" I say. I'm astonished . . . natch.

The guys are crowded around me, hee-hawing like a team of mules.

"How come empty?"

"The whole school's on a trip to Scummy Lake. Left before breakfast. Won't be back till bedtime . . ."

I hang up on her. We're all amazed. Bleary looks at Fergus. Fergus looks at Kleeger, Kleeger looks at me. We sit tight the rest of the day. Nobody sleeps. At nine o'clock we report for work. The days greet us outside—grinning like wolves. They throw the keys at us and disappear into the wagon.

We charge up the stairs . . . we chase through the bedrooms—we flick on all the lights . . . we're gasping—empty —not a soul—not a . . . Godamercy! Them sons of bitches!

Once again we foregather in the stairwell . . . we're morose . . . we grit our teeth.

Ah . . . what's that? A gurgling sound upstairs—a tremendous gurgling sound—utterly unnatural. We charge up to the lavatory to have a look. It's Pinsk . . . slowly, like a genie out of a lamp he emerges from the bubbling john . . .

"Gentlemen," says he up to his ankles in the pot, "let us pray."

I don't know. These Christian Scientists pull off some miracles. It's wonderful, the power of prayer.

Kleeger stabs at the handle, he's going to flush the fellow down again—

"Stop!" I cry. "Let him alone, Kleeg."

I've never been one for putting down resurrections. If a man wants to survive as bad as all that then I say: "Welcome back, Pinsk!"

Then everyone follows suit and there's a great deal of handshaking all around. Bleary breaks out the grog. We all have a nip. We have another. Pretty soon we're all out and Fergus takes a jaunt over to the package store down the road and comes back with a more festive quantity. An hour passes and we, even Pinsk, have degenerated into a mere heap of crockery.

"Irresponsible is what them day boys is!" declares Fergus.

"It was a rotten trick," assents Kleeger.

"Disgraceful," Bleary mutters.

"Godamercy."

The night wears on. It dissolves. It evaporates. The dark's a liqueur. It smacks of licorice. We gobble it up like nobody's business. Before you know it there's nothing left but light. And then the days arrive. It's the same story all over again. We vamoose the hell out of there and leave them with their hundred ghosts. And when we come back at night they retaliate in kind. So it goes. Night after night . . . dawn after dawn . . .

Years pass—centuries. Forever and ever the days and the nights exchange the same old forgeries, ghosts, the vaguest remembrances of a hundred runaways. Periodically Pinsk raises his hue and cry and gets flushed for his trouble down the john and shit upon, and rises again—the extreme vicissitude . . . he has not given up hope . . . someday, he feels, he will clog the drain . . . he's trying to put on weight. Daily I ring up Penelope—the answer's the same . . . one hears her scratching away . . . 'tis a percussive music . . . the broad expanse of her doololly straddles the horizon—one yearns toward it . . . one touches it betimes . . . it's feverish and hairy . . . it keeps one going. She visits me at nights now—at work—we've a hundred beds from which to choose . . . the ghosts are most accommodating . . . you'd be surprised how quickly they vacate the sheets once she slips into bed beside me—but she comes less and less frequently . . . one grows old. Penelope. . . . Penelope!

Mornings after work I go down to the river and give myself

to the fog . . . the fog is an obscure, a strange regality . . . it makes of me a mineral, rarefied and precious . . . it slips me round a finger and shows me off at fancy places . . . my eyes glitter. I do not see but I shine . . .

But I'm straying . . . straying . . . falling apart at the seams. The dark is deranged . . . the bit of sleep one steals of it is full of fits and starts . . . riddled with catastrophes, rife with visions . . . one sleeps laboriously.

On the Face of It

We lie on the beach, Thurston and I. Acne, it is bad. One despairs of ever getting rid of it. One lies in the sun, bakes. It helps. There are other cures, which one may take in a closed room, but they are expensive and dull.

My friend, like me, is on his back, his eyes shut, his palms turned up, abject before the sun. I have grown accustomed and indeed strangely fond of his odor and his voice. Thurston and I, we have a rapport. We have an identical misery and shall enter college together in the fall.

"Thurston," I say, "I am confident! No pimples come September. I feel it in my bones."

He sighs.

"Sometimes, Willy," he says, "I pray for cancer of the skin. Forgive me. I know that is irrational. Revolting! Yet, it would eat up the acne . . . and there is nobility in cancer. One is hospitalized, one is pitied, one dies of it. There is no humor in it. One attains dignity at last."

I do not answer. Poor Thurston. I have had the same thought. We are one, this fellow and I. We even look alike. Acne has so overwhelmed us that my features have become indistinguishable, or so it seems, from his. Eyes, ears, nose, and mouth—all are obscure, like those impertinent mountains that lie under the immense veil of pocks and scars on the moon. I do not recognize the moon by the shape or size of its mountains. All moons have the same face.

The girls, many girls, go by. One does not makes passes. One knows one's orbit. One looks, hopes . . . there is a force between us—

One prays for cancer, yes—but for clearness as well . . . for girls, many girls. Thurston and I, we have come of age. We are fantastical, but would at last realize in the flesh our fantasies. We desire . . . and now, we are determined also to be desired. We hope, we are optimistic—though we speak with bravado of cancer, we should in the end be displeased with it.

At noon Thurston goes to the refreshment stand and returns with milk. We toast each other's health, and I deposit the empty cartons in the wastebasket nearby. I must run to get to it and back. The sand is hot. I lie down again. We do not eat today. We drink milk, we lie in the sun, occasionally we talk. The day passes. A cool wind blows off the sea. We open our eyes; it is twilight, gray. We sit up and meditate the darkening waters. The crowds have gone. The lifeguard stand is empty, a thin chain locked across the front; the beach is officially closed. A few stragglers—two pairs of lovers and a large family . . . poor they seem, Poles I believe—gather their accouterments, shake their blankets in the wind, haul them in, and go away. The moon comes long before the darkness. . . .

We remain. Our lives are simple. Our homes are broken. We have been spared the complications of a happy childhood, a respectable family. No one worries that we do not return to our beds that night. We sleep beneath a white, a powerful moon, a cool breeze. I have brought two extra blankets, but Thurston refuses to use one of them.

"Do not expose yourself to the moon all night, Thurston," I say. "It is . . . unhealthy."

He laughs. I do not insist. I fall asleep almost immediately thereafter.

The sun alarms me in the morning, I sit up. It is early, the beach deserted. The lifeguard arrives and takes a swim. He splashes about impressively. He is strong, athletic, and young, though quite bald . . . a white man, handsomely bronzed. Most of the people who come to the beach are white. It makes no difference.

The lifeguard comes out of the water at a run, refreshed, vigorous, shaking the beads of water from him with obvious delight. He loves himself. He looks at us oddly for a moment as he passes. I merely smile—but the look . . . disconcerts me.

I turn to Thurston. He has become an albino—I had feared that. The moon. Just as I was dropping off to sleep I had said to myself, "The moon is dangerous and Thurston is vulnerable— we should not sleep here." But my lids grew heavy, I had not the will to take my fears seriously, and then, I do not as a rule trust them, my fears. I am cognizant of my weaknesses. I often, too often, exaggerate. I am inclined to believe in the fantastical—I am superstitious, I am young, impressionable. Yet, I have a great longing to civilize myself. It is difficult, a struggle. If one only knew which of one's fears to trust, then might one act with proper force.

Gently I wake him. He opens his eyes. They are pink and nearly blind, but he discerns me—I can tell—as a shadowy form. With a great effort of his spindly arms he pushes himself to a sitting position. He looks up at the sun for a moment. He winces . . . he sees nothing now. That first ray of light, so sudden to his already weakened system, was too much.

"Thurston," I say, "we must get you out of the sun."

"I am blind, Willy," he says. "It is no shock. I had a feeling all day yesterday that it would be so—do you believe that? You must!"

I reassure him that I do.

He continues: "And I must tell you, I am relieved. I am glad. I have always imagined that there was something leveling about it—and . . . now that it has happened I feel . . . yes, by God! I feel that I was right! It has leveled out!"

"Good," I say. "But we must go now, Thurston. The sun is rising. In your condition—"

The lifeguard appears before us. He puts a finger to his lips and gestures to me. I stand up and he whispers in my ear, "Is he, your friend—is he an . . . albino?"

"Yes."

"Then, don't you think you ought to get him in out of the sun?"

I motion to him, politely, to go away—indicating that the situation is in control and that I shall have my friend out of the sun shortly. He, the lifeguard, is satisfied with this, retreats a few yards, and watches with interest.

"Thurston," I say, "the sun will kill you. Let us go."

"I do not fear the sun," he answers, distantly.

"You misunderstand me," I say. "You are an albino, Thurston. You haven't a chance."

"Albino!" he says, and laughs. "Why, whatever gave you that idea! That's amusing!"

"But true," I say. "Just look at your skin!"

One forgets oneself.

"Forgive me," I say. "I forget."

"I believe you have sat in the sun too long, Willy," he says, smiling. "Run along, why don't you. Stay in the shade. You need a rest. As for me, I am looking forward to another splendid day on the beach. Yesterday did a great deal for my complexion. I can literally feel the acne shedding from my face. One more day, I believe, should turn the trick. Tell me truthfully: how do I look?"

"White as a sheet, Thurston." I am hoarse.

He laughs.

The lifeguard returns.

"What's taking so long?" he wants to know.

"There's a bit of a misunderstanding between us, sir," I explain. "My friend does not believe that he is an albino."

The lifeguard seems bewildered. Thurston continues to laugh.

"Believe me," says the lifeguard to Thurston, "you're an albino all right."

Thurston laughs again.

The lifeguard spins a forefinger in a little circle near his head, attempting thereby to indicate to me that he believes Thurston to be a lunatic, and says, confidentially, "That's just how they laugh."

The crowds are arriving. Up and down the beach, blankets and umbrellas appear . . . laughter, the odors of sun lotion and homemade sandwiches, of frankfurters turning on the grill at the refreshment stand; splashing in the water; babies cry. There are no clouds, no breeze. We are in for a hot day.

The lifeguard is beside himself. He must attend the crowds. The waters are rough, the people irresponsible. Life hangs in the balance. A drowning can cost him his job. And yet . . . there is Thurston. What to do?

"Let us say then, my good man," says Thurston, peacefully, to the lifeguard, "that I am indeed an albino, as you say . . . ha, ha! Well? What of it? I daresay there is not a single ordinance prohibiting the use of a public beach to albinos—is there? Of course not! Believe me, sir! I am acquainted with the law!"

"So am I!" says the lifeguard, matching Thurston's rather disgusting boast.

"Doubtless," replies Thurston. "I should say, in fact, that

you have the unmistakable voice of one who is intimately acquainted with the law."

"What do you mean by that?" asks the lifeguard, narrowing his eyes mistrustfully. "Are you putting me on, you lunatic?"

"Not at all!" says Thurston. "How should I? Me . . . a mere albino! Ha, ha! And blind! Insane, to boot! Where, my dear lifeguard, would such a creature as I acquire the cunning to deceive a formidable fellow like yourself? I am a crazy blind albino! With acne! There—I confess. I submit beneath the force and intelligence of your accusations, preposterous as they may be. Nevertheless, I am entitled to remain on the beach. And if you use main force to remove me, I assure you I shall have you to court . . . will see to it personally that your lifesaving certificate is revoked. I have intimate connections in the Red Cross."

"No kidding!" cries the lifeguard, confused, backing away from us, slapping his thighs, like a huge mad bird. "A big shot! Connections! The Red Cross!"

"Do get a grip on yourself," says Thurston.

"Go ahead!" cries the lifeguard, still walking backward and slapping his thighs. "Stay all day! Get yourself roasted! See if I care!"

"Thank you," says Thurston, coolly.

"You're not an albino at all! Okay?"

"Okay."

"You're black as the ace of spades! Okay? Don't even have to worry about a sunburn!"

"I'm glad," says Thurston to me, "that he has finally come to his senses. An albino! Did you ever?"

"I never."

It is difficult. I excuse myself and go to the phone booth near the refreshment stand. I use my last dime.

"County Hospital."

"Good morning, madam. I should like to speak with Emergency."

"One moment please . . ."

"Emergency. Miss Halisborg."

"Good morning, madam. My name is William Hangorf. I am at this moment in the phone booth of the Third Street Beach."

"Has there been an accident?"

"Several, madam—several."

"Drownings?"

"No, madam. There is a fellow here, a friend of mine, Thurston Weed, who is lately become an albino. He is also blind, and, I am afraid, at the edge of a psychotic breakdown."

"How old is he?"

"Seventeen."

"Has he previously registered with us?"

"Not to my knowledge."

"Bring him in. The doctor will have a look."

"You misunderstand. He refuses to leave. He has resisted even the advice of the lifeguard. If I may, I should suggest an ambulance, several competent attendants, and a straitjacket."

"Has he been affected, as yet, by the sun?"

"An excellent question," I say. "Yes, he has. Just before I left to make this call, I noticed long blisters, frightful, bubbling across his arms and legs."

"I'll send the ambulance right away. Third Street Beach."

She hangs up.

I return at a run to the blanket. The lifeguard is there. His hands are on his hips and he is staring, dumfounded. Thurston is nowhere in sight.

"Has he run off?" I ask, breathless.

He seems, this muscular beautiful man, in the grips of aphasia.

"Where is he?" I demand.

He points at the blanket. Thurston is there. One overlooks him at first. He has shriveled up and become a raisin.

"Ah, goodness . . ." I sigh.

The ambulance arrives. The attendants approach us.

"Where's the patient?"

"Gentlemen," I say, "we shall no longer require your services. Thank you just the same. You may return to the hospital. The patient you were sent for has become a raisin."

They exchange, these two attendants, a cunning smile, and wink once at the lifeguard, who remains unable to speak. They club me over the head. When I regain consciousness, I find myself strapped in a straitjacket in the lobby of the hospital. There is a dispute among several people going on. I open my eyes. It is a nurse arguing with the two attendants.

"Get him out!" she cries. "The man has a communicable disease. Goodness, you've been working here long enough to . . ."

She sees that I am awake, and she cuts herself short. She motions to them to release me from the jacket—a considerate woman.

"Sorry to inconvenience you, sir," she says, hovering, a voluptuous angel, over me.

"No inconvenience at all," I assure her.

"If you'll just walk on down a few blocks to the skin hospital, I'm sure you'll be much happier there—"

"Oh, no," I say. "You misunderstand. There's been a horrible mistake."

"I know!" she cries, almost in tears, and placing the back of her hand on her forehead. "I know!"

How pretty she is.

"You see, madam, I am in perfect health, both physically and mentally. I am not in need of medical attention. You have made an error in your diagnosis. I have a simple case of acne, a perfectly harmless and incommunicable . . ."

"Of course, of course—"

"It was my friend Thurston, alas, who was in need of your services. He had become an albino in last night's moon, and, I am afraid, a trifle touched—if you follow what I mean. But now he has shriveled up into a raisin . . . a hopeless case. There is nothing to be done. One of course might pray for his soul— would you do that, madam? That little thing, for Thurston? Silly proud Thurston? Would you pray for him—this Sunday?"

"Saturday," she says. "I am a Jew."

"Forgive me. Saturday then."

"Sir, I shall pray for the entire world this Saturday. If your friend Thurston was of this world, then be sure he will have been included."

"But that is the thing—don't you see? One can never be sure—about Thurston . . . that is, of which world he was. He was . . . so unpredictable, so fickle! One never knew what he would come up with next. A raisin! Can you imagine? . . . Wait. Did you say you were a Jew? How marvelous! So was Thurston! He had converted! Did you ever? It is inexplicable. But, there it is. He was a man fond, overfond, of the bizarre and the burdensome."

"This man," she explains to one of the attendants, as if I were no longer able to hear her voice, "has lost touch with reality and is no longer able to cope with or function in the everyday world. Take him to the front door and give him, as simply and clearly as you can, directions for getting to the skin hospital. It is less than a mile. He ought to be able to find his way."

They take me to the door and give me directions. I wander off. I think of the lovely nurse. How surprised I was to discover that she too, like Thurston, was a Jew. How well they would have got along together! If only . . . ah! Futile, these speculations. But she was lovely. Wasn't she lovely? Pity my acne hadn't cleared up a little more. There might have been a chance, a . . .

That is a fine word. Futile. How I love to say it! It rings, rings like a bell!

I walk by the skin hospital. It is painted white. I go in. I say, "I am William Hangorf. I should like a private room."

"What is your complaint? Have you seen a doctor?"

"I have no complaint. I am perfectly satisfied. I should like a rest, that is all. I have not seen a doctor."

"I'm sorry. This is not a rest home. I might suggest one of the hotels."

"Oh!" I say. "Wait! My acne!"

She laughs. There are serious diseases in this place, truly communicable and devastating. Acne is nothing here, laughable. One is humiliated and leaves. I wander the streets. Night falls. I have not eaten in two days. I am mad with hunger, with friendlessness. I find myself at the beach, the moon is full. My blanket remains, untouched. I sit down on it. The sea is calm. The waves rustle gently, like dry leaves in the wind. I pick up the raisin between my thumb and forefinger.

"Thurston," I whisper, "can you hear me?"

"No," says he. "I cannot hear you."

"Good old Thurston! You haven't changed a bit, have you!"

"No."

How small his voice is, though. How very small.

"And your complexion—ah, it is bad. Your skin, it is scarred and pitted . . ."

"Yes, but there is great goodness," he says, "in this lacerated unrecognizable body of mine."

Goodness.

I flip the raisin into my mouth. I have been hungry too long. I do not believe in asceticism. No, there is enough suffering and denial in this world. Let us be joyful! The fruit is sweet; my hunger, for the moment, is assuaged. There is a pit inside. I bury it in the sand.

"May you rest in peace, my friend. Forever—by the sea . . ."

The moon brightens, the beach is bathed in a light fiercer than the sun. There is no yellow in this light, no color at all—only white, and perhaps a touch, but a faint, a delicate touch, of blue.

Out of Thurston's grave a vine comes and creeps wanly across the sand, branches everywhere. It winds about the life-guard stand and climbs up and down the stone wall beyond the dunes. A million Thurstons—albinos, and men with acne, and many mutants and exotic hybrids blossom, loosen themselves, and drop naked off the vine. They segregate into armies and all, except the albinos, enter the sea, and crawl over the waves—south, out of sight, to the equatorial waters.

"Farewell!" I cry. But they do not hear me.

The albinos, nearly blind, nod like old men at one another, and at nothing, and wander aimlessly up and down the shore. They are looking for shelter, I believe. One of them it seems has discovered a cave mouth in the jetty. He enters and the rest follow. As the last one disappears into the rocks, I leap to my feet and go after them. I shout into the cave, but they do not answer. There is a moan that goes among them, but that is all.

Throughout the rest of the summer I see them, occasionally, when there is a full moon, stumbling and nodding over the jetty. It is not a pleasant sight. The vine withers and is soon obscured by the shifting sands. I enter school in the fall. My skin clears. I am popular. I graduate. I am elected most likely to succeed.

But what do I do with myself? I am haunted by Thurston. I

return to the jetty and become friendly with the albinos. They are suspicious at first, but eventually accept me. I do my best not to antagonize them. I do not go into the sun anymore; this would embarrass them and they would find reasons for being angry with me, and I do not want that. I must be faithful to the one friend I have had. These albinos are his legacy. I feel somehow that he has left it, most especially, to me. I must therefore treat them with respect. I have begun to take up their mannerisms—I nod, I stumble about . . . deliberately. My eyes are not so good anymore and, with each passing day, become more accustomed to the darkness of the cave. Of late the glare of the moon hurts me, hurts me bitterly. Blindness comes on . . . it will be a relief. My arms grow thin as theirs, out of disuse. There is little activity. They cannot stand it, poor creatures.

Thurston, I have been true to you. I have even taken one of them to wife. She is a good woman with a short life span. I do what I can to please her.

I think continually of those others that grew out of you, my friend—those that have taken to the sea. Most likely they have been devoured by the prodigious monsters that one encounters out there. Had they reached a continent and established a colony, one should certainly have read about it in the news-papers but there has not been a word.

A Thief in the Temples

Once it starts, there is no stopping it. First it goes at the temples, then at the crown, it dries at the nape and around the ears, and eventually the dome is revealed, clean, clean as a whistle. A slow process. Better Delilah. Have at it in one go and forget. It is the dragging out of the whole business that gets you down.

Maniconi knows all about it, a specialist. "Vanity is my business," he says, just as bold as you please. He makes no bones about it; he lays it on the line and lets you know he is a quack. Everybody buys: some because they are convinced inevitably by bad acting, and others because they would like to beat him at his own game. "Okay," they think, "it's a fake. But what if the fake, just one time, works? Won't that be something? I guess he'll laugh out of the other side of his mouth, that phony."

The man has photographs all over the walls—a vindictive mob, mostly from the stage and the silver screen. They beam down at you, the stars, as if to say, "Tough luck, baldy," and each one has a few lines of prose across the shoulder: "Thank you, Maniconi, for making my hair gorgeous again," and other saucy variations on the same motive. It gets your back up. That is part of the game of course. Humiliation.

As for the customers . . . it is a sideshow—at every turn one encounters another silly configuration of one's vanity. One never knew it could take so many shapes. They are all in attendance. Step right up. No obligation. Pay as you leave. There is a certain amount of trust. Maniconi, he can afford it, trust. If you don't pay, you don't leave. Everybody pays. You don't want to commit yourself for more than an hour to a place like that. You would rather be outside, out there in the big tent, where most of the people you bump into have enough brains at least to keep their fears and fallibilities under their hats and scare up as many idiotic diversions as possible.

I sit in a chair before a mirror and Maniconi's assistant rubs my scalp; she is a Swedish woman in middle age; the scent of the secret formula drifts about us; she leans against my back and occasionally she hums. This lasts about twenty minutes, then she dries my hair and I proceed to the outer office where Maniconi is bent over his desk. Maniconi is a formidable figure. His back is crooked and he trembles as a result of a famous disease; his moustache is waxed; a black string is attached to his glasses and looped around his neck to prevent their dropping to the floor when he trembles too much and they fall off his nose; he wears an excellent wig of straight black hair—one does not mention the wig; it is a fact universally disregarded among his clients. I give him ten dollars and he forces his trembling hand to write a receipt.

"How much longer do you think it will take?" I ask.

"If you like, you may discontinue treatment at once. You have made excellent progress."

"I don't notice the difference."

"Ah, you must ask your friends . . ."

"They tell me I'm getting balder every day."

"They are blind. You have blind friends."

"Perhaps I should get new friends, right?"

"That is not necessary. In two months—that is, if you continue treatment—you will have a head of hair the virility of which will be unassailable."

I give him a certain smirk by which I let him know that he is full of it; then I take my hat from the rack. An old man enters as I leave. Maniconi, in the beginning, was in the habit of saying, "You see that old man? He's a doctor." All right. One of the tricks. A doctor believes in the secret formula. Even Maniconi cannot afford to dispense entirely with the sanction of the AMA.

It is a bright day out. A young lady gives me the eye. I am not bad with my hat on. We wait side by side on the street corner for the light to change. I ought to tell her right off, "It's you, lady, you and your kind, that makes me spend twenty bucks a week on this futile crap and sweat blood when I see my hair fall, the dandruff piled in drifts everywhere I go . . ."

"Excuse me," I say.

Suddenly her face is all aflutter, like a tree on the first day of spring, and she says, "It's green."

And so it is. Green. We cross together and by the time we reach the other side we are laughing, mainly because in truth it was red, not green, and she is a trickster; a hand, a lovely hand, is holding the crook of my arm.

"Let's have a drink."

"Splendid," she says.

I take her to a sidewalk café, so that I can leave my hat on without seeming too out of it.

We have a couple. I make a date for that night and rush off home. Angus is already there, most likely. I'm late. Everything happens at once. The first time in my life I pick up a girl and Angus pops up to jam the works. Two years. He might have waited one more day. I knew it was a bad omen, felt it in my bones, I remember, as soon as I'd opened the telegram.

DEAR DADDY
TWO YEARS LONG TIME NO SEE 3 PM
MONDAY JUST LIKE OLD DAYS
ANGUS

He is waiting for me on the stoop in front of my house. He waves at me and grins like a shark. He too is wearing a hat.

"Hi, Daddy!" he cries.

He is a sick man, is Angus. I allow him the liberty of calling me Daddy, but I let him go no further. My best friend, he says he is. We were thrown out of divinity school together. They caught him peeking one day at my exam paper, of which I, rake that I am, let him have an unobstructed view. We have been brothers of the underworld ever since and my life has become one shady deal after another. I'll skip the details. I work for an organization and free-lance on the side.

I carry his suitcase for him up the stairs. We sit facing each other in the living room. Angus leaves his hat on. So do I. We don't talk much at first.

"Take off your hat, old buddy. Make yourself at home."

"Thanks," he says. "Rather keep it on. I'm very sensitive to head colds these days."

"It's nearly a hundred degrees. Don't be silly."

"How about yourself?" he says, slyly.

"With me it's different, Angus. I've become a ritualistic Jew—hats, separate dishes, the works."

He laughs.

"Please," I say. "Leave us not make light of this thing."

"Far be it from me," says he. "It's just a shock, that's all. A good Lutheran like yourself. Whatever got into you?"

"I can't say exactly—it was a feeling . . . I had a religious experience. You know how those things are."

"Sure."

"One morning I woke up with my hat on."

"Amazing."

"And I said to myself: 'It's a sign. What does it mean?' "

"Fantastic."

"Then I went to the kitchen . . . the ham had disappeared from the refrigerator and there were mezuzahs nailed on all the doorposts."

"Pretty clear, wasn't it—"

"Not the shadow of a doubt," I conclude. Luckily the fellow who lived here before was in fact a Jew and failed to remove his mezuzahs from the doorposts.

I show Angus his room. He is understanding about my date. "Go ahead," he says, "far be it from me . . ."

Philomena and I go to a café and then walk. It is imperative that we stay outdoors. Though she invites me up to her apartment later, I have unfortunately to turn her down. Tomorrow night I will take her to a discreet stretch of beach and hats on we will have it out.

Angus is asleep when I return home. I get my flashlight and go to his room to have a look, but he is still wearing his hat, the fox. Very gently I work it up off his head and hide it in the closet. The next morning at breakfast he is mighty upset, and suspicious.

"This doesn't look like the regular sort of burglary, old buddy," I say. "I don't think anybody would go to all that trouble just to steal a hat that has been slept in. I mean, nothing else is gone—I checked. If you ask me, it's another sign."

"Miraculous place you've got here," he says.

"I know. It gives me the creeps."

He is unconvinced, I can tell.

"Looks like you're losing your hair, Angus," I say, as offhandedly as I can, but he is all at once terribly upset.

"Don't sweat it, Angus. There is a cure for all our ills. Come on—"

Hesitantly he follows me out of the apartment; I lead him through the town; there is a strong breeze today, and his few strands of hair blow this way and that . . . it gives him a demented look.

"Where are we going?"

I return him a little excruciation, a cabalistic smile, for an answer. We proceed up the stairs to Maniconi's. At the sign on the door, Angus turns white. I smile at him and we enter the outer office.

"Maniconi, this is my friend Angus. I thought you might like to have a chat." I wink.

Maniconi takes his cue and escorts Angus into the inner office. I go get the routine rub from the Swede, return to the outer office and read *Look* magazine. Then out comes Angus, pale, with Maniconi grinning to beat the band, and the two of them repair to the treatment room. After a bit Maniconi comes out alone and pats me on the shoulder. "Thanks," he says.

When Angus at last reappears, he reeks; his hair is plastered down and black with the fabulous oils; he looks balder than ever and his face is drawn and sickly. He puts a ten dollar bill on the desk. On the way home I try to make him talk, but in vain. He looks at me as if I were one of those impertinent photos on the walls—I don't like it—and as soon as we get back to my place he sticks his head under the tap in the kitchen.

"You're not supposed to wash it out till tomorrow morning," I say. But what does he hear? The water rushing down over his ears and spinning in the drain.

I sit in the living room and read the paper. I look at the newsphotos. I tabulate how many of the bald-headed men are good guys and how many bad. It is fifty-fifty, really. Murderers, athletes, politicians, rapists, thieves, columnists—you can find us in all fields of endeavor. We have to make an extra effort. But how many of us are handsome? There's one! A movie star!

Sure, a few. There is always hope. Losing your hair doesn't necessarily put you out of the running. The major thing is not to let it get the best of you. It is the anguish that goes along with the opprobrium of this comical affliction that makes one ugly in the end—the sour look one gets on one's face, the worry lines, the nervous warts and pimples that spring up out of the depths of frustration, the pouches hanging like the flags of ignominious defeat from the sides of one's jaw . . . you have to keep your chin up.

The water stops rushing in the kitchen. Angus comes in, a towel slung over one shoulder; his hair is dry; it looks better dry. He throws the towel onto the couch and goes about getting his things together, then waits, suitcase in hand, by the door. All right. I know what he wants. I unlock the closet and give him his hat. He nods.

"What's the rush?" I say.

A tear trickles out of the corner of his eye. "I'm disappointed in you, Ambrose," he says.

"That's a hot one."

"What got *into* you all of a sudden? 'That Ambrose,' people used to say to me, 'he is all soul.' But now you are all body. What changed you?"

"My hair fell out."

"No," he says. "Some spiritual catastrophe drove you to this. Tell me about it."

"It is very simple, Angus. One day I looked in the mirror and said, 'Hang it all, I'm bald as a bean!' That's the sum of it."

"Come, come," he says.

The superiority of this prig is hard to take. Besides, this isn't the place at all for such talk. Mrs. Schammelweiss the widow, my neighbor, peeps out at us now and again and then slams her door in such a way as to let us know that she exists too but doesn't care to join in the conversation because she is too busy going out of her mind with boredom in her apartment. This is a point to consider, and, in all fairness, to appreciate. Her hair is falling out too—that is the gist of it. It must be a hard thing for her to live with, especially now that strangers are talking about it, her affliction, in front of her door.

Angus turns and walks away from me. He pauses at the head of the stairs.

"See you around," I say, and start to go back in.

"What have I got left?" he mutters under his breath.

"I don't know, Angus. What have you got left?"

"Nothing!" he bursts out . . . at last. He pounds his forehead with his fist. "There's nothing of value!"

"Buck up, old man," I say.

Mrs. Schammelweiss has opened her door, without reservation now, her wretched face shining with curiosity and wonder before the weeping abomination who has appeared so unexpectedly in her dismal hallway.

"Humanity has let me down," he cries, in full voice, "God has let me down, and now . . . you, too! You, Ambrose, were my one hope! That thread, silver and strong, which tied me to life. Daddy, it has snapped. I feel myself tumbling into the abyss—chaos, despair—help me!"

"I'm sorry I'm not your silver thread anymore, Angus. But you'll find another. Look around. Why don't you get married or something?"

Mrs. Schammelweiss cackles.

"Who would marry a man like me?" he cries, "I am bald at twenty-three! There are no bald women anymore and the hirsute . . . they are incapable of . . . understanding our problem! They laugh! Even a dwarf has a better chance! He can marry another dwarf! What should I do? Tell me!"

"Buy a wig!" snaps Mrs. Schammelweiss and she slams her door. I do likewise. I listen at the keyhole to him sobbing and muttering as he descends the stairs. The front door slams; I go to sleep; I wake up; it is almost night; the phone is ringing.

"Hello."

"Is this Ambrose Bean?"

"Yes."

"I have a message for you."

"Oh?"

"I am Neil Fender, a cousin of your friend Angus. He killed himself this afternoon. He left a note for you. I'll read it. 'Dear Ambrose, I absolve you. Forgive me for expecting you to be better than you really are. Yours in eternity, Angus.' "

"Thanks," I say.

"Is that all you've got to say?" says Cousin Neil.

"How did he do it?" I ask.

"I don't know. The body hasn't been found."

"Then how do you know he's dead? Maybe he had second thoughts."

"Not likely. Angus was a man of principle. He always kept his word."

I hang up. I have a date; I have to shower and shave. Cousin Neil sounds curiously like Angus.

I'm beside myself.

I pick up Philomena about eight and we repair to the beach. And then, around midnight, here I am, naked, and done to a turn, with my hat on, lying on my back, and I'm thinking, "Let's make it a permanent arrangement." I can't keep my hat on forever, and she is bound to chuck me as soon as she catches me with it off.

"Let's get married, Philomena."

"When?" she says.

"Tomorrow afternoon. I'll meet you at the synagogue at one."

"Synagogue! Are you a Jew, Ambrose?"

"Of course! What'd you think?"

"But I'm a Lutheran! I'll have to study up—"

"Don't worry about a thing. Just be there at one. And bring a bonnet."

Fast, fast! Quickly! Don't stop to moan!

I'm a Lutheran, too. So what! I'll convert. Lutherans don't wear hats in church. One look at the light beaming off my nut and she would run back up the aisle so fast that . . . what? It would be embarrassing, I can tell you. I would nail myself to the pulpit then and there. No, the Jews have the right idea. Hats. And don't tip it, not to anyone, not Caesar—not the King of the Universe even.

Early in the morning I go have a chat with the rabbi, to set it up. I have heard about him—a chiseler, not thought much of by the congregation. There is a rumor in the wind that he will be out of a job as soon as they can find a replacement. He gets pushed around from temple to temple; he has been at this one only three months. The gossips have it that he has been married twelve times, and is working on his thirteenth and fourteenth simultaneously, with a Chinese mistress into the bargain, a Buddhist. It takes nerve.

The temple steps are flat and low, dirty, chipped. It gives you a good feeling to take them two at a time. Wait. Here comes Maniconi out of the vestibule. I skip backward down the steps and duck behind a pillar before he spots me. He has a shaky walk. What was he doing here? Saying his prayers in this place, that humbug? More likely collecting bills. But from whom? I have a notion.

Except one old man, the rabbi I take it, the place is empty. He is seated up front, one arm embracing the chair next to him. A telephone is harnessed to his shoulders by wide black straps. The extension cord is thick and long and it snakes across the temple, disappearing under the door to a chamber off to the side of the ark. There are no pews in this place, just folding chairs. The floors are bare; rotten pine; the air is fetid; everything is old, old; it gives your stomach a turn; there are cobwebs on the rafters; the light is bad, yellow; the walls, like a withered map, with white plaster islands floating in a dark, dismal ocean, are cracking everywhere. The messiah has not yet come and they let you know it right off; the whole room is rank with that fact.

The telephone rings. "Yes?" says the rabbi. "This is he. I am speaking to the Presbyterians on Monday. Perhaps another time. The same to you." He hangs up.

I touch his telephone and he turns and squints at me . . . all lies show themselves in the end! So this is Maniconi's idea of a doctor, is it. A fine physician. He looks me up and down; there is a faint light of recognition in his eyes, but then it fades.

"Rabbi," I say, "I have a problem. Can you spare a few minutes?"

"Minutes?" he says, smiling. "That's easy."

He leads me into a chamber off to the side of the ark and we sit facing each other.

"I have to get married today," I say. "Can you do it?"

He is puzzled.

I continue: "I'm not a Jew, you see. But my fiance, she has to marry a Jew—d'you understand?"

"Yes. Her parents are pious."

"No, no. She is not a Jew either. She is a Lutheran, like myself."

"Interesting."

"Her parents," I say, "have always wanted her to marry, as they say, a Jewish boy. They have a great, one might say a psychopathic, admiration for you people. If only their daughter marries a Jew, they think, then everything will be all right. It has something to do with business."

"Business?"

"Her father has gone bankrupt thirty-one times—and always because he has been outwitted by his competitors, all of whom, of course, are Jews."

"I might recommend a psychiatrist—"

"No, no. He is quite sane—"

"Eh?"

"Besides, there is no time, not a second to lose."

"She is pregnant?"

"Nine months gone."

"And why did you wait so long?"

"I don't know! Forgive me, Rabbi!"

The telephone rings.

"Yes? This is he. I am speaking to the Catholics on Tuesday. No. On Wednesday I am speaking to the Baptists. Another time perhaps. The same to you." He hangs up and looks me over.

"Do you mind if I smoke, Rabbi?" I say.

"Please do. I'll join you."

He reaches for one of my cigarettes. Good. He is low on tobacco.

"Well then?" I ask, after a moment. "Will you marry us?"

"It is highly irregular," he says, quite dogmatically—but he is not thinking about irregularities; he is thinking about the wonderful smoke, like holy spirit, filling his lungs.

"I would be willing," I say, leaning forward a bit, "to make a substantial contribution—"

"Contribution?"

"Shall we say one hundred dollars—that is, in addition to the regular fees and whatnots?"

He is silent.

"There's very little time remaining, Rabbi. She was already in the early stages of labor when I left her an hour ago."

"The first birth is always a drawn-out affair. There is plenty of time. Believe me, I have been through these things before— many births, many wives . . ."

"Well then?"

He gets up and puts one elbow on the windowsill. The light turns his face pale. "I should not like to be giving you Lutherans a false impression of my people," he says, looking out at the street. "We cannot be bought, you understand."

"I never . . ."

"I would have to lie to my congregation. That is hard. But, after all, they have been lied to before, have they not?"

"I suppose they have!" I say, cheerfully, and I wink.

But he returns me a sour look; he is not in jest. "Then again," he says, "one must ask: what is a lie?"

"Precisely," I say. "It's relative."

"No, it is absolute. You must understand that," he says. "However, I am deeply moved by your story. Clearly the situation is urgent and calls for an immediate decision. Moreover, your offer is most generous indeed. But—what shall I do with this money of yours? Though the temple is sorely in need of repairs, the truth is that one hundred dollars will scarcely put a coat of paint on the walls."

"If it's not enough—"

"Then again, the ram's horn has disappeared just recently. In a few weeks we shall have need of one, because, you see, we are approaching the High Holy Days—"

"I see."

"You do not see at all."

"That is, of course, what I meant."

"You see, with part, only a part, of your hundred dollars, I can purchase, if I am so inclined, a new horn. However, though

I can purchase a new horn with even only a part of your hundred dollars, I shall not do it."

"No?"

"The horn is dispensable. We, my congregation and I, have heard it before, many times. We are well acquainted with the sound. Our imaginations, this year, will suffice."

The telephone rings. "Yes? This is he. I cannot. I am speaking to the Episcopalians on Thursday. The same to you." He hangs up.

"Whatever shall you do with the hundred dollars?" I ask.

"If I took it," he says, "I would give it to the messiah."

"Good idea, Rabbi," I say. "So it's all set. How about one o'clock then?"

He turns from the window and looks at me. "You think I am a fool, don't you?" he says. There is a pause. "Why don't you ask me," he continues angrily, "how on earth it is possible to give money to the messiah!"

I begin to stammer a reply, but he interrupts. "The messiah has an office downtown," he says, looking at me significantly. "Occasionally he drops in at the synagogue for a visit. In fact, he was here just before you arrived. You missed him by only a few minutes."

"Just my luck," I say. "If only I hadn't missed that bus!"

"Perhaps you passed him on the street."

"What does he look like? A cloud of smoke?"

"Not at all. He is quite human. He has a black moustache, spectacles, and his body quivers in the most extraordinary way—"

"I'll keep my eyes peeled."

"You do that," he says, smiling into his shirtfront, "And when you find him, throw yourself at his feet . . . if he favors you, he will see to it that through his good offices you transcend the ravages of time. True, he has appeared in a most bizarre and unexpected shape. He has, it seems, no respect for tradition. Then again, how foolish and unconvincing he would have been if he had appeared in servile accordance with the prophecies."

"Rabbi," I ask, "do you preach this messiah in your temple?"

"No. I am not at liberty to. The messiah has not as yet seen fit to accept me."

"Accept you?"

"He has set me a trial, you see. The day that I can show him that I have grown one new hair on this withered head of mine, then, he says, he will believe that I believe. You see? It is very sad. I am wanting in faith."

"But only the messiah himself could grow new hair on a head as old as yours."

"Precisely. I cannot grow the hair until I am saved by the messiah. The messiah, however, who is greatly fond of paradox, will not save me until the hair is grown. I shall therefore, my young friend, give him your hundred dollars in the hope of compromising him. Perhaps he will take pity. What do you think?"

There is a knock at the door.

"Come in," says the rabbi.

The door opens. It is Maniconi. He looks us over and smiles. "My two prize patients," he says.

The rabbi is disconcerted. The telephone rings. "Yes? This is he! I cannot! On Friday night I am speaking to the Jews. Forgive me!" He replaces the receiver on the hook and stares at Maniconi defiantly.

"I returned," says Maniconi, with sardonic composure in spite of the quivering, "merely to apologize. I have made an error in my calculations. Your bill, Rabbi, comes not to $25,357.00 but to $25,358.30. You will excuse me, I am sure. I have human frailties and am subject to error."

He bows and leaves, shutting the door behind him.

The rabbi looks at his hands. "So," he says, "you too . . . ah well. And now you know . . . but what can one say? It is most embarrassing."

"Please, Rabbi, there is no need to be embarrassed."

"But there is! Don't you see? This business of being bald has taken almost complete possession of my brain! Really! I scarcely think of the messiah and the rest of it at all! Is that not shameful? For me the messiah is . . . what? A horn—you'll forgive me—an old broken lovely ram's horn—into which one can spit a few tunes. Heaven on earth . . . the idea is so remote that one can only nod one's head over it. The important thing is that the more hair one has, of course, the more profound does one's nodding appear. What, I ask you, is the nod of a bald-headed man if not a comic episode? I have become infatuated with appearances. Take off your hat."

He leans forward and motions at me to show him the top of my head, which I do; he clicks his tongue. "Bad, bad," he says. "And at your age . . . a pity. Wait."

"What?"

"Everything is becoming clear! What preposterous lengths a man will go to! Eh?"

He laughs a long time until the laughter dries in his throat and he begins to cough; then he twinkles at me, and says, "Your real reason for wanting a Jewish wedding is that you don't want your bride to see that you are bald—correct?"

I nod.

"That is a mistake," he says. "Look at the sorry pass I myself have come to . . . listen and learn, my friend! I too was a Lutheran." Whereon he throws his arms around my neck and weeps on it; we embrace; we recognize one another; nothing more need be said.

He eases back in his chair. "Yes," he sighs, "I had wanted only to cover my head—do you see?—just like yourself! And then, I discovered that in order to do so, I must cover all of me. I walked into the sea, as it were. The water became deeper and deeper, and once it had at last covered my head, I was not able to continue to keep it covered until I had resolved to forsake the air altogether and accept water, this viscous medium, as my permanent habitat. And here, in water, one must learn everything anew. One must learn to breathe with one's gills, to see with one's eyes closed, to walk without touching the ground. It is entirely bothersome, and, frankly, impossible. Why in the world I am still alive I do not know. But, of course, I am. How could it be otherwise? Do you dare propose that I am dead?"

"I never—"

The telephone rings. "Yes!" he cries. "I shall be there! Send someone to pick me up! Next week!" He hangs up. He looks at me. He says, "The Town Council of Priests, Rabbis, Ministers, and Monks . . . they are killing me. Do you see? A slow death. This telephone . . . one of their regulations. It was proposed and approved the last time we convened in Geneva. Every member shall wear a telephone. The straps dig into one's skin, do you know? And then they are always calling one up. It is bad for the posture. Look! I am bent under the weight of it. Communication, do you see? They are trying to eliminate misunderstanding—well and good!—so that some day we can see that everybody is deep down saying fundamentally the same thing and that we are all in the end Roman Catholics at heart! I wish them success. We are making great strides. The Pope has recently forgiven the Jews. Great strides . . . killing me, killing me!"

The door opens and a Chinese beauty appears. "Do not come to see me tonight," she says. "Never again. I have found another rabbi. He is kinder and better looking. He has a beautiful head of hair." She leaves and shuts the door.

"Forever!" cries the rabbi.

The door opens. It is an old man. "We have found a replacement, Rabbi," he says. "The pressure has been too strong—from the congregation. And then from the Town Council of Priests, Rabbis, Ministers, and Monks, too. They say that your speeches are those of a madman. You perpetrate a false impression of us. We Jews are not mad. The new rabbi will be installed in the morning. Peace." He leaves.

The door opens. It is nobody.

"The wind." The rabbi rises and shuts the door. "I'm tired," he says. "I cannot. No, I cannot. The pain. Enough! One must seize the bull by the horns. One cannot wait forever. I must have money! Peace! Women! Hair! On my head! Which I cannot grow! Until the messiah who is never coming comes! And then it is *still* uncertain whether or not he will find it necessary in this kingdom of his to eliminate baldness . . . a moot point. Listen to me, listen to me! The Town Council—I must annihilate it! Every church! Without discrimination! A nonsectarian coup! Stop interrupting! I have a plan. Give me a cigarette."

He lights up, seizes me by the shoulder, and begins whispering and blowing smoke in my face. He has a provocative plan.

"But how do you get in?" I say.

He pulls away from me, amazed. "Don't be foolish! Do you think I have practiced this filthy trade and been a member of the Town Council of Priests, Rabbis, Ministers, and Monks these thirty-seven years for nothing? I know the combinations, my friend! The combinations!"

"Rabbi, I'm with you."

Whereon he extricates himself from the telephone and leaves the chamber, motioning excitedly at me to follow.

I catch him just as he is about to pass through the vestibule to the street. "Where are you going?" I ask.

"Why, to the churches! I thought we understood one another!"

"Aren't you forgetting something?"

"Eh?"

"You mean to say that the synagogue has no money in it?"

He laughs, rather nervously. "Ah well," he says, "not much. Hardly worth the risk."

"How much?"

"Pennies. Let's be off to greener pastures."

"How many pennies?"

He nods his head at the floor and exhales profoundly in defeat. We reenter the synagogue and descend into the basement. He unlocks a little tin box with some paper money and a lot of coins in it. "One hundred seventy-five dollars and change," he says. "The profit from last week's rummage sale."

We stuff the box with newspaper and leave the coins. Then we are out, hurrying down the street together. The sun is bright, the trees along the avenue are in full leaf, all the world is smiling upon our venture. We hit the Roman church first.

"Rabbi," I whisper as we pass through the pillars, "take me by the arm."

He does. His head is thrust forward, his pace is quick. The pews are immaculate, the aisles are like chutes to the pulpit, the soles of your shoes echo on the stones; there are shafts of scarlet and green and gold among the shadows—it is a tunnel, this place, standing on its end.

"Now there is an architect for you, Ambrose. Do you see? Up there. He has designed parallels that do in fact meet. Impatient. He could not wait for nature to turn the trick; a matter of cutting expenses. However, should an angel ever try to descend through the point at which these parallel lines meet, he would run up against a stone wall. But they are innocent of themselves, these Catholics; no malice intended. They put their fingers on the apex and they say, 'Wonder of wonders, these lines really do meet! Hallelujah.' What can one do?"

"Take me to the vaults, Rabbi."

He laughs, cunning, Jewish, among the arches of the Goths.

He pulls me along; we follow the plumbing to the cellar; he kneels before the vault and deftly, deftly, turns the cylinder; he knows the numbers, every one, and when to turn it clockwise and when to turn it back. The door swings out; the vault is agape; a thousand, a million green tongues flutter at us in the dark. What to do with all of it?

"The supermarket," says the rabbi, breathlessly. "Get some paper bags, some cartons."

I hurry up out of the basement. I walk cautiously up the aisles; stone figures catch one's eye unawares from eerie places. How empty it is! Where are the mourners, the priest? And where is the man who keeps the place so clean? It is he, above all, whose presence is most clearly divined everywhere—a phantom custodian sweeping the light out of the darkness, dusting the pews, the crucifix, the magnificent silver head of the microphone on the pulpit.

The market is like the day before Christmas. The shopping carts clatter, the cash registers are incessant, like a sleigh ride; women and children are bouncing brightly colored packages about; two nuns and a priest contemplate an orange. A bagboy presents me with two cartons and a stack of paper bags. It is a fine shock of hair he has. I tip him and return to the rabbi.

"Quickly, quickly!" he says. We make short work of the vault and leave a penny inside for good luck; we ascend the stairs. A young priest accosts us as we are making our way up the aisle; we put down our bundles in a nearby pew and greet him respectfully. "We have been on a shopping trip this morning, my nephew and I," says the rabbi, "and we have come into your beautiful church for a little rest. It is so cool in here. Truly, Father, some day I may convert."

"But of course, Rabbi, you're not serious," says the priest.

"I am!" insists the rabbi. "Do you think I want to burn in Hell? No, I tell you, I have been giving the entire question a

great deal of thought lately. The . . . how does one say it?—
the 'Old Testament?' It no longer suffices. Do you see? It wants
a culmination. You must drop around and see me."

"I would be delighted."

"Shall we say a week from tomorrow?"

"Excellent," says the priest, restraining the corners of his
mouth from breaking into a triumphant smile.

We hire a cab and we hit the Lutherans next—then the
Methodists, the Baptists, the Presbyterians, the Episcopalians.
The Mormons alone give us a run for the money. Their vault is
the biggest of all. A guard sits in front of the lock, a well-
dressed man in his twenties or sixties. He is reading a book on
agriculture. We ask after his health and depart.

"The Mormons have always managed to outwit me," says the
rabbi. "God is an American—do you know? They are too
original; I don't know how to speak to them."

On the way into the wig shop he whispers, "Here you will find
the very best. Strictly exclusive. They don't sell to Jews. These
are people with refined sensibilities."

The proprietor is a funereal dandy in his forties; the rabbi
addresses him grandly. "Sir, today I am celebrating the occasion
of my baptism. I am, you will be pleased to know, henceforth a
Christian. The water is, in fact, not yet dry on my brow.
Therefore I have come, together with my godfather here, to
exchange this dusty hat for an elegant wig."

"Allow me to shake your hand," says the proprietor. "May I
ask your Christian name?"

"Benedict."

"And you, sir?"

"Ambrose."

"And what, may I ask," says the proprietor, turning to the
rabbi again, "did you have in mind?"

"The very best."

"Then you have come to the right place."

"A pair of blond, shocking blond, wigs is what we require—is that not so, Ambrose?"

"Yes. Blond."

"And as for the price range—?" asks the proprietor.

"Price, sir, is no object."

"Excellent, my dear Benedict. This way, please."

We follow him to the back of the shop where he shows us a rubber bust with thick, straight hair, a scarcely perceptible wave.

"Now this little item here—"

"Lovely."

"Notice that the individual threads of hair seem to be springing from the follicles of the skin itself. This wig, gentlemen, is attached hair by hair. It is not, as the common run of wigs, a mere rug, so to speak, that one lays across one's head. Moreover, these hairs do not turn gray, they do not fall out, they are waterproof, washable, and do not wither in arid or windy climates. In short, a wig which on the one hand imitates nature, and on the other surpasses it. Ten thousand dollars."

"Very good. We will take it. Unless, of course, you have something better to show us . . . ?"

"My dear Benedict, there *is* nothing better, believe me. Not in the entire world—the universe, if I may be so bold."

"You may," says the rabbi.

One by one the hairs are plasticized into our heads by the proprietor himself—he has a little machine which resembles a soldering iron.

The cabbie smirks as we pile into the back seat.

"Okay, wise guy," I say. "What's funny?"

He plays deaf. "Where to?"

"Go on," I say, and lean over the back of his seat. "Pull it."

"What's that?"

"My hair."

"You're kidding."

"Pull it."

He does. "Hey! That ain't no wig!"

"That's right. It's the real article. Get it? We were wearing rubber balloons over our heads before. Now step on it. Third and Barnabas."

We pause, the rabbi and I, on the landing before Maniconi's door, gather our separate solemnities, don our hats, and push on in. Here he is, racking up his accounts at his desk; we have caught him unawares.

"Mr. Maniconi," I say, and I manage to squeeze up a tear or two for the event, "permit me to kiss your hand."

He is taken aback; I press his quivering fingers to my lips before he has a chance to assemble his nerves. The rabbi follows suit. We take off our hats.

"It's a miracle," I say.

Maniconi ceases to tremble.

"Mr. Maniconi," says the rabbi, "you have outdone yourself. Truly, this is apocalyptic, is it not?"

With caution Maniconi approaches me, lifts his hand to my head, lightly touches the wig and pulls at the hair, but he can scarcely believe his fingertips. He goes to the rabbi and tugs at his hair, too. He begins trembling again, whirls around, and shouts for the Swede.

"So you've got yourselves some wigs at last," she says, laughing in the doorway.

"No, Olga," says Maniconi. "Listen to me. Those are not wigs! This is hair! Grown by you and me! And the secret formula! Touch it! You'll see!"

The rabbi counts out thirty-one thousand dollar bills and lays them on the desk.

"This should cover my bill, including a little extra, as a small token of our appreciation. Sir, suffice it to say, we are grateful."

But Maniconi is not listening.

"What exactly did you do to these two the other day, Olga? Think! Perhaps some slight change in the treatment . . . ? Come . . . we must begin immediately!" He tears off his wig. "Closed till Christmas!" he cries. "Put a sign on the door! Everything . . . I want you to do everything to me that you did to them, Olga! Try to remember! We must write everything down! Nothing is to be overlooked! Even if it takes us a hundred, a thousand years!"

"Five thousand," says the rabbi. "Five! Five!"

Maniconi disappears into the treatment room. Olga tacks the sign on the door and flies in there too, bumping into Angus, though, at the threshold, who is on his way out. He looks fine, really. A sojourn in the grave sometimes does a fellow a world of good.

"No need to blush, Angus." I say. "You never had me worried for a minute. I'm glad to see you've come to your senses. Maniconi will solve your problem, believe me, if you stick with him long enough, like I did. Believe in him with all your heart, Angus, and one fine day, you just wait and see, you'll wake up with a head of hair as fine as mine."

I smile and with a rakish toss of the head flip the resplendent hair off my forehead. The rabbi and I leave. I don't want to hang around too long. Angus will get an account of the miracle anyway sotto voce from Maniconi, be sure of it. I'm not about to let him in on the facts . . . why should I? A fellow has to suffer through these things and find out for himself. He would have it too pat if I let him in on the wig shop now. Circuity, procrastination—they stretch life out and fill up one's history. Without them you have straightway arrived at your destination, and then where's the adventure?

The rabbi and I leave. We walk the streets arm in arm, hatless. We have a half-hour to kill before one o'clock. It is fine to be a blond when the sun is out. You get the feeling it is honest work, belaboring the pedestrians to take notice of something in this world.

At one I meet Philomena on the temple steps. The rabbi waits in a bar around the corner. She looks fine today. The plan is to take her to Brazil with us on the evening flight and marry her there.

"You know, it just occurred to me, Ambrose, that I have never seen you with your hat off."

"Really?"

"With hair like that, I can't understand why you keep it covered so much of the time."

"Oh well, I don't like people staring at me."

"Oh Ambrose," she says, her eyes filling with tears, "I love you so . . . Do you realize how much I love you?"

"Sure."

"Ambrose, I *want* you to realize."

"Okay."

"I would sacrifice everything—everything! Just to please you!"

I have never seen her like this. I ought to tell her about Brazil right away, before she goes off the deep end. It is the finality of marriage likely that has upset her so.

"Listen, Philomena—"

"Oh, Ambrose! I must tell you about what a . . . lovely time I spent last night!" Her shoulders are shaking and I put my arm around them. "I spent the night at my girl friend's apartment. Elsie. She is Jewish and we stayed up all night talking about what it is to be a Jew, and . . . oh, so many things! And it was just beautiful, really! What beautiful people the Jews are, Ambrose. Oh, I'm so happy, so happy! And she read me the Bible. Whither thou goest I will go? It's so beautiful, Ambrose! I want you to be proud of me. And my people will be your people—do you remember? AMBROSE!"

Her neck is taut, her eyes are wild. Not pretty, not pretty. I
let go of her. She rips her bonnet off, and brandishes it, like
Judith with the head of Holofernes. She is bald; she is desperately triumphant and quite exalted by the horror of her pious
deed. "I did it for you, Ambrose! Do you believe me? I love
you!"

"Listen, Philomena, there is a fellow I want you to get in
touch with—his name is Angus. He is a friend of mine, an ex-
Lutheran like yourself. He has been to divinity school and
knows the ins and outs. He will tutor you for the conversion. I
had a chat with the rabbi, you see, and he suggested the
marriage might be a bit premature. You need to study, he
thinks. Remember? You suggested that yourself. Meanwhile this
Angus fellow, he will make a good bridge. And then, in about
three weeks from now, we'll have the wedding. That is the way
the rabbi says it ought to be. I think he's right. What do you
think?"

There is a great to-do. I put her in a cab and slip a handkerchief to her through the window. What now? Ring up Angus at
Maniconi's.

"She loves bald-headed men, Angus. But you'll have to
convert. She has set her heart on a Jewish husband. I'd talk
mainly about the Bible at first until you have created a little
pedestal on which to establish your intimacy. Tell her you're a
Jew, a convert."

They ought to hit it off just fine, the two of them.

I take the rabbi to the barber for a shave, and forty years of
beard are shed upon the linoleum. His face is pale, pale, and
smooth, soft as an infant's. It has never touched the blade
before. We each buy a sharkskin suit and a plane ticket. We are
passing through the clouds hung over the West Indies.

"Where are we, Ambrose?"

"Over the wing."

"Yes. And in a few hours? Rio de Janeiro—blond and rich.

Did you notice the stewardess? She is Latin. She has been
flirting with me; watch her eyes. These Latins, they are infatuated with blonds. Ah, my friend, all these years! And what for?
It would have all been so simple, so beautiful! I am tempted,
Ambrose, to discover a purpose in it all. And believe me, it
would be quite simple for me to demonstrate by way of rhetoric
that there was indeed a purpose, that my life had to be lived in
this way and no other, and that it was all for the best and that
this glorious culmination to my life would have been impossible
without all that had gone before. All nonsense. I will not justify
my life. What do I care for justification at this point? Am I not
over the wing? Does the reflection in the window not tell me
that I am young? There, you see? My face floating across the
southern skies! But how can such a beautiful face be mine? It
cannot; therefore it must be an angel's. You see? I am laughing
at myself. That I can laugh at myself, however, does not prove
that I am ridiculous. On the contrary! So, you see, it is a net. I
have enough courage to dismiss summarily the Council of
Priests, Rabbis, Ministers, and Monks; but to dismiss the
angels—that I can never do. There is a skullcap on my brain, a
prayer shawl draped over my lungs, and the philacteries are
wound about the vessels of my blood. Out of myself, that is
where I long to go. Brazil? A second best. Ambrose, I must tell
you, I cannot stomach Latins."

He goes on, in a circle; dialectic and dissatisfaction have
become necessary to his digestive tract. I let him rave. After
this, what more can you do? He plunders the coffers of his own
synagogue, all the churches, shaves, gets a wig, flees the country, deserts his family, even buys a sharkskin suit, and still he
frets about angels. How is that? I don't answer him and he falls
asleep. Right. When there is no one anymore for him to argue
with, he nods off. What will he do in Brazil? Are there Jews
there? Anywhere? He will end up bickering in the marketplace,

my little rabbi, haggling over a pound of coffee, the ripeness of a banana. He dies in flight; after we land, I sit awhile and let the plane empty. No one is left but me and the stewardess; even the pilot has gone. The motor is off; there is peace; the earth is not moving.

The stewardess approaches and looks at us, oddly.

"He's drunk," I say.

"Is he a friend of yours?"

"Oh, we exchanged a few words on the trip, but I don't even know his name. I suppose you have a problem on your hands." I take my suitcase and leave.

My passport is in order. Cries of ecstasy rise in the air, louder, ever louder, as I make my way to the heart of Rio. They are bearing the rabbi along the wide avenues. The procession is grand, festive; the sun is bright; little girls swoon about the coffin; the bearers are tall, Indian, with a stoic madness in their stride. There is music, trumpets. "Prophet!" is heard from all quarters. It is the face they love—this old man, so still, so peaceful, sweet as a child. But why are they doing this? It is less than an hour since I left him on the plane, dead, unknown, a public nuisance. What an odd turn of events. I make inquiries, but you can hardly get a sensible answer. "Why? Because he's beautiful, that's why!" Beautiful. These are great lovers of beauty. Maniconi prospers in this part of the world. One sees the signs. Amazing new secret formula. He has branches in every sky. His agents are using the occasion for an advertising gimmick; there is a little sign on the coffin: "This is what Maniconi can do for you." What is it exactly they mean by that? It is obscure, but effective; no doubt, these fellows know their public.

I wander conspicuously through the crowd. Women stroke my heart with the lashes of their eyes. I am apparently in great demand now among the dark races—but tomorrow, even greater.

The Sheriff

My posse had capitulated to the outlaws. I was alone and in despair. I say alone, but there was my horse, and she was a faithful beast; though now even she grew sullen and refused to allow me on her back. She followed behind me, sniffing the ground at my heels. Whenever I spoke to her, she stopped walking and closed her eyes. There had been no water for two days, no water. I could see their tents on the hillside, and the smoke of their fires. They had water, and food. I knew they could see me. I was the only moving thing in the desert, I and my horse. I held a white flag. I knew they would not kill me if I held a white flag. That is the way with them. That is their code. And they will never break their code, for they are the most unimaginative of men. I am the last imaginative man. I know all of the codes and find this knowledge most useful. When I arrive at the camp I collapse. The outlaws bring me water and crowd around me, laughing. But the men from my posse do not approach and will not look me in the eye. They are not cunning, these fellows, and have remained just as foolish outside the law as they were inside it. I shall take no small pleasure in the supervision of their hanging in the village square.

"Gentlemen," I say to the outlaws (I had to address them as

a group, for they had no leader—why should they have a leader? They were all of them nitwits and in perfect agreement on every subject), "Gentlemen, you have been clever. You have outmaneuvered me. You have lured my posse from me with food and drink—then you left me to die of thirst in the desert. But there is one thing you did not understand; namely, that my thirst for water does not equal my thirst for justice."

Which made them laugh.

"You laugh," I continued, with a severe countenance, "but you see, I am not joking. Look behind you, gentlemen. You are surrounded."

Still smiling, they turned their heads casually this way and that. I said, "Surrounded by trees, gentlemen." Then they roared with laughter, roared. They thought it a wonderful joke.

One of the men from my posse stepped forward timidly and ventured to remark, "I'm glad to see you haven't lost your sense of humor, Sheriff." He winked at me.

But I did not look at him pleasantly in return. I looked at him in silence, so that he turned and withdrew at once, like the sheep that he was.

Bald Ben, my deputy, then steps forward, grinning ironically. What has taken him so long? He is never at a loss, this one, and thinks himself different from the others—but he is not. The fact of the matter is that every one of them thinks himself different from the others; therefore, even in that respect they are alike.

"You ought to have given up when the rest of us did," says Bald Ben. "What has your steadfastness got you? A sick horse, nothing more. And look at the poor beast. She almost died out there, Sheriff. I tell you this: it will be a cold day in hell before she lets you in the saddle again."

All eyes turn to my horse, who is lying now on her side in a swoon and breathing noisily.

"What right have you to talk to me of my horse?" I say to Bald Ben. "You, of all people!"

"No right," he says with sardonic composure. He delivers me a theatrical, contemptuous smile and repairs alone to his tent. I do not call after him. I say nothing more. There will be reparations soon enough. I will have to be content now, to bide my time.

In the evening a tent is prepared for me, and a guard is posted outside it. I retire early, after a pleasant dinner. I lie on my back and rehearse my predicament. My pistols have been taken from me, my horse is sick, my posse has deserted, I am a three days' journey from town: it is even conceivable the outlaws may kill me—if not out of bloodlust, then out of boredom. If I could persuade one of the men from my posse to see things from my point of view, perhaps there would be some hope. But why should they see things from my point of view? They have never had it so good. They have deserted their wives, their work and their tiresome duty to the law. They spend their days and nights now in these luxurious hills and want for nothing. They even have women here, fine lusty girls, ensconced on the other side of the stream. Moreover, when the idle, carefree life becomes tedious and the men grow restless for adventure, they have it. They ride into a village and indulge themselves in the most vigorous of styles. A fine life. And I envy them, these weaklings. Perhaps I myself ought to join them. What would it take? A word, a friendly smile, a handshake, nothing more.

But they would entertain suspicions. In the back of their minds they would imagine I was double-dealing. This would cause tension, which in the end would cause them to kill me. These fellows are not accustomed to tension, to doubt; they cannot handle it. I know them.

Besides, I could not live happily with such people. They have stolen the mail, a full week's mail. For this I can never forgive them. Perhaps I might make an effort to discover where they have hidden the mailbag and abscond with it. But where would I go? Hiding in the hills—which are surrounded on all sides by desert—would be futile. Eventually I would have to cross the desert. And in the desert, no matter when I cross it, I am visible.

No, what I need now is ammunition. Somehow I shall have to take their bullets and their pistols. And then, the only armed man in the camp, I shall issue threats and ultimatums, making of them an orderly submissive crowd, and drive them before me through the desert. Otherwise there is no hope. The poor honest citizens will be forever defenseless against the onslaught. All of the able-bodied men of the village were members of the posse. Who remains? The old, the lame, the blind, the pious, one entrepreneur, the schoolteacher, the minister—and women and children. Who will defend them now? With my posse dissolved, I am like a figurehead without a ship.

In the morning I wake to sounds of laughter. I emerge from my tent. The outlaws are gathered at the crest of the hill. Merry and excited, slapping one another on the back, all talking at once, they are pointing at something on the desert. I join them, the guard following close at my side, and am greeted robustly. "Look, look!" they cry, and several of them put their hands on my shoulders and bring me forward.

In the distance one can see a wagon train crawling toward us. There are twelve Conestoga wagons accompanied by a multitude of people on foot and horseback. A spyglass is thrust into my hands—it is the citizenry of the village! There is a white flag flying from every wagon.

Clever. A clever, courageous gesture on the part of these simple folk. It brings a tear to my eye. I must admit, I never thought they had it in them. Apparently they have conceived a method of attack similar to my own: an obsequious approach.

Yet, it makes me sad, sad. It seems I have been called to witness a merciless slaughter. These poor people have never handled a gun in their lives. They are accustomed to the peaceful trades, and to the quieter modes of justice.

The wagon train climbs the hill and halts at the entrance to the camp. Seven old men come out of the lead wagon and approach us. A delegation of outlaws is dispatched to meet them. A conference ensues. The old men are highly animated and make emphatic, desperate gestures with their hands. They speak in whispers. The outlaws are listening gravely, rubbing their chins. The rest of the outlaws, with grim foreboding, join the conference. I am not allowed to join. I grow weary. What possibly can require so much talk?

When at last the conference disperses, I approach the outlaws, but they have all assumed an introspective air and turn their heads away from me. The seven old men, however, are hobbling excitedly back to the wagons, babbling incoherently and gesticulating madly. In response, a unanimous shout goes up from the citizens, and then all at once the wagons overflow with women and children, the equestrians dismount, and the entire populace, laughing and weeping for joy and crying, "Bravo, bravo!", rushes into the arms of the outlaws—who are overwhelmed and puzzled. Some of them are smiling sheepishly, but not happily.

Automotive Immortality

My car is not ready. It will never be ready. The mechanic is a thief. I am certain of it. But there's nothing to be done. No proof. I cannot assert myself. I cannot bring forth accusations because I do not know how to make myself understood automotively. The soul of a car is more incomprehensible to me than all the souls of India. I am familiar with the term "carburetor." I know it resides under the hood, the fabulous hood. But I could not locate it, nor do I have a notion of what it looks like. It has something to do with gasoline, but what exactly I cannot say. Right now the carburetor is of no consequence anyway. The mechanic says that the carburetor is all right. That is of course a lie. The very root of the trouble is undoubtedly located precisely there, somewhere in the phantasmagorical confines of this carburetor. The mechanic is a thief. I know for certain that the mechanic is a thief because he was recommended to me by a friend.

An hour ago my car had a nervous breakdown on the road and had I not at the time had the presence of mind to turn the key off it should certainly have gone entirely to pieces under me. I immediately called my friend Farnsworth.

"Hello, Farnsworth? What shall I do? I am on the highway. I

am blocking traffic. I am miserable. Neurasthenia has finally got the best of the Edsel."

"Call VQ9-0767. Ask for Fritz."

I call Fritz and presently he arrives upon the scene in a strange red truck with an immense fishing pole jutting from the back. The line is as thick as your fist. A whale hook dangles from the end. I shall not tell you what he, this Fritz fellow, does with this hook. It is too fantastic. You would not believe it. Suffice it to say he manages to drag the Edsel to his lair. Though I ride in the red truck with the mechanic, and proffer many interesting and friendly remarks, he says nothing. He is dark. He is in a greasy study. He says nothing. He is insolent and reeks of the underworld. He is a fool! A fool! I will surely strangle him. I am sitting now in his hideout. He ignores me. Several times I have asked him in the most courteous manner what is ailing my poor car. But he does not condescend to answer. I am not there, I am nowhere, nothing. Only once did he answer. It was when I asked him about the carburetor. "No," he said, "not the carburetor." If only . . . ah, if only I knew the names of some of the other parts! Then perhaps I might establish some rapport with this Fritz. Who knows? Perhaps he is not such a bad fellow after all.

I approach him. I have been sitting here one hour and six minutes. I am anxious. He is charging me by the hour. He is charging me five and a half dollars by the hour. That is an impressive figure, true enough, and yet I would not object to it were he giving my car his undivided attention. But he is not. He is a busy man. The telephone has rung eight times since I have arrived. Once it was a wrong number but every other time the party was loquacious. Fritz however was most businesslike and economical in his speech, I'll have to give him that. He did not seem to be wanting to waste his time and my money on the telephone. But his customers are all apparently chatterboxes and chew upon his ear. They are meddlesome. What do they need to talk to him about? Can't they simply tell the man their car needs fixing and then leave him to his business? No, they must always be pestering, pestering! I will surely strangle one of them. But the telephone . . . the telephone is not really what galls me. It is the fact that Fritz is constantly walking away from my car and dipping his head in other cars too. He spends no more than seven minutes at a time with my car and then he spits and looks at another car. And all the while I am paying through the nose for this—for the telephone calls, for the other cars, for the spitting. So you see it is understandable that I am anxious and annoyed as I approach him, and yet I have delicate and refined sensibilities and therefore I display a chivalrous style upon addressing him.

"Ah, Fritz," I say, "if it were only the carburetor. Then it would be so simple, eh?"

He answers with a curious gesture which I take to be a sign that somewhat vaguely, if profanely, concurs with my subjunctive ecstasy. I am encouraged and press on: "Tell me, Fritz, what would you venture to say it might be?"

He looks at me. I am penetrated, annihilated. Then he speaks: "The whole fucking transmission is shot to hell."

"Forgive me," I say. "What is this—how do you say?—fucking transmission? Will it cost very much to repair? In our country we know very little about cars. Some of the more progressive people have begun to take an interest and learn. But I—alas!—I have always been hopelessly atavistic!"

His eye scans me, like a finger across a map.

"Where are you from, buddy?"

"I told you: another country."

"*What* country, *what* country?"

This is most embarrassing. I am standing here before this creature who has just asked a really very simple and inoffensive question, and yet, for some reason, I cannot answer him. It is as if that glance of his had petrified a part of my brain. I cannot for the life of me recall where I am from. Where am I from? From another country. Of that much I am certain. But what country exactly I cannot say. I am terribly embarrassed. I reach for my wallet. I have some identification in there. The wallet is gone. Fritz . . . Fritz undoubtedly has stolen it.

"My wallet is gone," I say.

He says nothing.

"If I do not find it I shall not be able to pay you for your services."

Still he says nothing. His silence accuses him. It is all clear. He is in collaboration with Farnsworth. I must be cautious.

"Tell me, Fritz, why do you ask where I am from? Of what interest precisely is it to you?"

He spits. He turns away. He goes to the telephone. It is all quite clear. He realizes that I am aware of the entire affair. He is obviously trying to get in touch with his superiors for further instructions. Aha! For the moment I have confounded him. I have upset his plans.

"Own up, Fritz!" I shout. "It was the carburetor all along, wasn't it!"

He looks at me askance over his shoulder. He is whispering nervously and rapidly into the receiver. He hangs up. He picks up a huge wrench and faces me.

Ptoo! I spit at the floor. "You filthy pig!" I am in a rage.

Ah . . . what's that? Sirens? Yes. Sirens in the distance. They are screaming and Fritz is smiling. He is pleased. The sirens are screaming and he is pleased. He is a pig.

"Perhaps we can make a deal, Fritz—eh?"

"Deal? What kind of deal?"

"You fix the Edsel and I will give you eighty-four thousand dollars. But you have got to fix it before those sirens arrive."

"Make it eighty-five."

"All right. It is a deal."

He runs to his workbench, throws something under the fabulous hood and shuts it tight. Then he opens the door and starts the motor. The sound is wondrous, symphonic! I am laughing. Fritz opens the door for me. I grasp the wheel joyously. He is holding my necktie in his fist, however, and his upturned palm is under my nose.

"It was the carburetor all along, wasn't it, Fritz?"

"Yeah, you guessed it, you old fox. Now pay up."

I reach into my jacket pocket and insert my poisonous-dart blower in my mouth and blow the lethal missive into his chest. I drive out of the huge doorway and start making—as they say—the getaway.

In the rearview mirror I see the sirens approaching. The lovely sirens. They are coming nearer and nearer. They are coming out of the sky. The lovely sirens with the long flowing hair and the voluptuous bodies. They float out of the sky and come at me out of my rearview mirror. Alas! And I am totally alone. There is no one to lash me to the steering wheel. I am gone, gone forever. They are carrying me away, away down the highway and across the vast hayfields into the sea, the green sea. My Edsel has become amphibious—which is no doubt due to the new carburetor that poor Fritz installed so deftly, may he rest in peace. I have achieved the impossible: automotive immortality. No wear, no tear. I am driving now the eternal car. The wheels float upon the waves and the motor is silent and while one siren blows the spray from the windshield another holds me in her arms and all is peace and precision and I drive the green seas forever.

O and I sat at the table for two days over that one. At the end I was exhausted and I thought, "Where is the profit in it?" I am told that the game must always end in a draw, once the formula is known to both opponents. But that is only partly true. I know the formula, and so does O; we learned it many years ago, as children, but the fact is that when we come to sit down at an actual game and there is money at stake, and dignity—and not only our own but the dignity of the game itself—then the formula flies out the window like a pigeon.

What good was that? There was nothing in it for either of us.

"O," I said, "we have got to introduce another player; otherwise we will never get anywhere. He will liven things up. Through him perhaps we may learn something, and progress, and make some profit."

O agreed wholeheartedly. So we introduced B. I am not sure where he came from.

"The alphabet, like everyone else," he told us; but I didn't trust him; he was different from O and me. And even though we assigned him the same value as we assigned ourselves, and made him abide by the same rules, he had some kind of an edge over us; though it is difficult to put one's finger on what it was exactly, that edge.

We let B go second in the first game.

```
X│O│O
─────
B│B│O
─────
X│B│X
```

We were disappointed, I must say, but gave it another try.

```
O│B│O
─────
X̶│X̶│X̶
─────
B│B│O
```

O and I began to laugh like schoolboys, and the three of us went out and had cocktails. I paid, and didn't mind at all, frankly. It is the custom for the winner to pay, and that is a wise custom.

However, we were all eager to get back to business, so we went up to my place and commenced.

Out for drinks we went again, and this time O paid. We were feeling good, but then I started to think, "Maybe B is an unscrupulous person who is deliberately letting us win so that we can be buying him cocktails all night."

Which proved me wrong, of course. He played brilliantly in that game. This dissolved my doubts about him, and both O and I shook his hand cheerfully, accepted him in our hearts as a friend, and we all went out and had cocktails. We had a high old time. When it came time to pay the bill, however, B said that he was sorry but that he had no money, and that he made it a rule never to carry any because he didn't believe in it. This threw O and me into a pensive mood; we split the bill between us and went back to my place. We all sat down at the table and I could feel the anger welling up in me; I hadn't said one word to B since the cocktails; suddenly I stood up.

"I know what it is that you are up to," I shouted. "Please excuse us, sir. O and I can get along well enough without you."

B smiled like a villain in a melodrama and, without replying to my outburst, walked out of the room. This only infuriated me further. But O exhorted me to get a grip on myself, and once again we commenced.

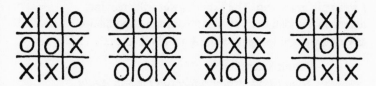

It went on for days like that—months and years. Both O and I grew thin and weary. We were growing old. We seldom mentioned B again; it was a painful subject and we tried to avoid it. Occasionally he would appear at the window, though, and smile at us in a subtle way.

Portrait of the Policeman
as a Young Artist

I will walk in the sun. The Eiffel Tower will greet me,
tell me in Turkish the way to Afghanistan. Apollinaire
& Vergil will guide me, because I am blind . . .

—Frank Kuenstler
from *Blind Ossian Addresses the Sun Again*

Robert Ennis declared himself a sculptor and left his wife and
three children in Toronto with a brief note. He went to Miami
with a pretty girl who had quit high school that year to be an
Arthur Murray dancing instructor and had a connection in the
underworld. Robert Ennis had been a policeman in Toronto
and very much admired. He used to walk his beat with a certain
air.

He liked this girl he had run away with, and also the feel of
stone. He intended to make both figurative and abstract sculptures because he was against all dogma on principle. He took
with him a duffel bag which contained toilet articles, one change
of clothes, and eighty-five pounds of tools. He had thirteen
dollars and change when he arrived in Miami because he left his
wife the $937 in their savings account and also the $264.08 in
their checking account. It was his desire to go to Jamaica. At
first he wanted to go to Haiti but was dissuaded by certain
persons who told him that there were politics there. He was tall
and had a Scottish nose.

In Miami he accepted the hospitality of the family of one of the dancing instructor's girl friends, a plump envious girl. When he first arrived, he had told himself that it would surely be through the goodwill of this family that his trip to Jamaica would be financed, because he noticed at once that they had in their living room a print of one of Paul Gauguin's Tahiti paintings. He loved the women in the painting and also he loved the watermelons, and he thought that certainly after he had told his hosts the story of the artist, passage to Jamaica would be a matter of course. But he was a poor storyteller. He didn't understand that a storyteller ought to tell his audience a story which they can believe in, if he wants them to give him money. Or perhaps he did understand this, but didn't understand what sort of story his audience could believe in. In any event, he told them about Paul Gauguin, but they could not believe in Paul Gauguin, or even the print on the wall, and they folded their arms over their stomachs like certain gunfighters in films about the American West. Undaunted, Robert Ennis proceeded next to tell them stories of his experiences on the Canadian police force and he even showed them a photograph of himself in uniform. However, they did not believe in Canada.

He remained in this house fifteen days. Every evening after dinner he and the dancing instructor sat on the floor in the living room and did exercises. First they did a set of exercises he learned in the Royal Canadian Air Force and then they did a set of exercises he learned from an Indian expatriate in Toronto who was referred to as The Master. Meanwhile the girl friend sat on the sofa and gave Robert Ennis provocative looks and her parents lay in the bedroom watching television and drinking cocktails and frowning at the wall whenever there was laughter in the other room. In the mornings he rose before dawn, took an enema in accordance with the principles of hygiene as enunciated by The Master, and after breakfast the girl friend drove him in her white Pontiac to one or another of the small craft harbors on Biscayne Bay or the Miami River. He hoped to find a boat owner who was planning a voyage to Jamaica. He looked for two weeks, but in vain.

On the fifteenth day a money order and a brief letter arrived from the dancing instructor's connection in the underworld.

> Dear Dolly,
>
> Here is enough money for one—I repeat: one—plane fare to Jamaica. It is for your boy friend. You come back to Toronto.
>
> Digs

Dolly showed the money order and the letter to Robert Ennis and confessed that she had written Digs for money last week. Robert Ennis was morose. He went for a walk, but returned in half an hour, took Dolly in his arms and said that he had a plan by which he might succeed in purchasing a plane ticket to Jamaica for her as well. He said that he would go to an airline ticket office and make a proposition: he would buy one ticket if they would give him another in exchange for a piece of sculpture that he would send them in a month from Jamaica. He said that he had a friend who was a painter and paid his dentist and doctor bills in this way. So Robert Ennis and the dancing instructor and her girl friend drove over to the Pan American Airways ticket office on Biscayne Boulevard.

The two girls waited in a soda shop while Robert Ennis went in to outline his plan to the ticket lady who told him to write a letter to the president of the airline. Then he was dejected. He went out the door but was followed by a man who had been sitting in the corner of the ticket office reading a flight schedule. He stopped Robert Ennis in the street and introduced himself as Mr. Corrington.

He was old, in his mid-eighties, but sprightly, fat and sunburnt. He had white hair and wore an expensive tropical suit and a yachting cap, on the front of which was a golden eagle.

Mr. Corrington said that he couldn't help but overhear the

conversation with the ticket lady, that he had sympathy and admiration for young artists and that he would like to help.

He said that he himself had had artistic aspirations as a youth, but that the world was very much with him. He said that he had gone into business immediately after graduating from college and had worked himself up into the presidency of a company which manufactured tractors and other heavy construction equipment. He said that he had retired only a few years ago. "Now I deal a little in silver, you know, to keep myself occupied with something. It is very boring. Really, you would be doing me a great favor by accepting the few dollars for your plane ticket." In return he asked only that Robert Ennis send a small piece of sculpture from Jamaica after he had settled in. "But there's no hurry about that. A year, two years . . . I intend to go on living for quite some time. Like Bertrand Russell, you know. Are you acquainted with Bertrand Russell? Great mind, that Russell. Do you know a book of his called *Nightmares of Eminent Persons?* Read it."

"I will," said Robert Ennis.

"Do you know who you remind me of? Paul Gauguin, yes. Something in the eyes. Do you know the self-portraits? Also you remind me a little of Brancusi, and a little of Degas as well . . . do you know the little sculptures of Degas? Ah, *trés elegant,* if I may so express myself. And yet? Degas, Brancusi, Gauguin—they are all quite different from one another. Then how is it that you remind me of all three of them!"

Robert Ennis smiled inwardly and shrugged his shoulders. "I don't know."

"Perhaps it is simply that all artists have a special quality in common—something very feminine and yet very masculine at the same time. In any event, you have that special quality in my estimation, and I am an excellent judge of character. That, you might say, is my talent: judging character. Oh, I was a very good businessman, I assure you. The only thing you lack is—

how shall I put it?—confidence perhaps? Yes, confidence. Am I right? Well, it will come . . ."

Mr. Corrington had little cash and no checkbook with him at the moment. They arranged to meet in a half hour in the lobby of the McAllister Hotel. Mr. Corrington said that he was flying to Caracas that night and had a few preparations to make.

Robert Ennis returned to the girls in the soda shop and he insisted that before he tell them the good news they all go across the boulevard to Bayfront Park. But once he had sat down between them in the shade of a banyan tree he felt like a stone and it suddenly occurred to him that the girls might not believe his good news. He looked anxiously from one to the other and he knew that he must take care to tell his good news with a right attitude and from a proper point of view.

But he could not decide what attitude to strike or from what point of view to proceed. He was besieged suddenly by a large crowd of points of view and attitudes and they all kept colliding and embarrassing one another like skaters on a pond, and he began to be afraid that his good news was destined to come off just as badly as the story he had told about Paul Gauguin. Therefore he permitted himself only a few cryptic remarks.

"I've just met a man with a golden eagle on his cap," he said. "Everything is going to be all right."

When the girls asked him to elaborate, he simply smiled. This approach was quite successful. The girls were frustrated, but credulous and expectant, and he continued in that vein until he went off to keep his appointment at the McAllister Hotel.

Mr. Corrington, arriving a few minutes late in the lobby, apologized extravagantly. He said that he would take Robert Ennis to the bank and cash a check immediately but that he had to inquire at the desk if there were any messages.

When he returned from the desk, he was holding a slip of paper which he had got, apparently, from the clerk. Then he said he had left his eyeglasses in the room, and he asked Robert Ennis to read the note aloud. It said: *Ready for shipment. We close at one. Gold & Silver Shop.*

It was now 12:45.

"Oh my." Mr. Corrington struck his forehead. He excused himself and disappeared into the elevator. In five minutes he returned with an attaché case in hand. Smiling as he passed Robert Ennis, he said, "It will take only a minute." Then he disappeared into the *Gold & Silver Shop,* which adjoined the lobby of the hotel.

He returned shortly, sat down, paternally touched Robert Ennis's hand, which was on the armrest of the chair, and said, "The silver has to go out this afternoon but they cannot take a check for the delivery and insurance. I will never get back from the bank before they close. It cannot wait until tomorrow because I fly to Caracas tonight. I have twenty-five dollars in cash but it will cost nearly one hundred and thirty."

Robert Ennis immediately gave him one hundred and five of the one hundred and seventeen dollars in his wallet and Mr. Corrington again disappeared into the *Gold & Silver Shop.* At a quarter after one, Robert Ennis looked into the shop, saw the decal on the glass door which said *Hours: 10 a.m. to 6 p.m. Monday through Saturday,* and went in.

"No," said the proprietor, "I don't know any Corrington. But a white-haired gentleman did pass through here about fifteen minutes ago. You say he dealt in silver?"

"Yes."

The proprietor winked. "Do you, perhaps, deal in silver?"

"No. I am a policeman. From Toronto."

"I see."

Robert Ennis returned to the girls with tears in his eyes and Dolly telephoned the police who found Mr. Corrington within the half hour. There was a confrontation in the police station and all but four out of the one hundred and five dollars were returned. The police said that they picked up the old man about twice a month; they knew his address and his haunts; they evidently took him for a harmless person who no longer has the wit to win at the games of his youth but continues to play them anyway from force of habit. They were amused by him as one is amused by a mischievous child and gently persuaded Robert Ennis to drop charges.

Mr. Corrington stood all the while in the far corner of the room, holding his hat in both hands. His posture indicated patience, irony and humility, and his eyes were vacant and sad, like those of a man who hears voices but does not understand the language. Robert Ennis had boasted to Dolly about the dynamic person he had been taken in by, and therefore was embarrassed by the figure Mr. Corrington cut in her presence.

Smiling philosophically as he shook his victim's hand, Mr. Corrington said, "Hard times make hard people," and Robert Ennis later remarked while seated between the two girls on the front seat of the white Pontiac that this was a fine adage and that he had begun to perceive a design.

But the design was difficult to articulate; he said that some day he would try to express it in stone. The essence of it, however, was that he believed he had made a covenant with the underworld.

He believed that his acceptance—previously unwitting—of this covenant was manifest in several significant acts: the declaration of his allegiance to art, the renunciation of his role as a defender of the law, the desertion of his family and the departure from his homeland. Also he had received money from the dancing instructor's connection, Digs—in short, from the underworld itself. However, the fact that this money was given conditionally made necessary the intrusion of a second underworld agent: Mr. Corrington.

Mr. Corrington was of course connected with the dancing instructor's connection (connected in the sense that all agents of the underworld are connected; their connection being the effect of an infernal cause operating independently of individual designs and deliberations), and he had appeared in order to punish the supplicant for his transgression of one of the conditions attendant upon the gift of the plane fare; which condition being that Dolly was to return to Digs in Toronto. The reason behind this condition was quite painfully clear: Dolly was to return to Toronto not that she might satisfy Digs—although that certainly would be a secondary consequence—but rather that Robert Ennis might be alone with his art.

It was now clear to him that any further attempt to avoid the conditions dictated by the underworld was futile. He told Dolly to telephone Digs for her plane fare to Toronto, borrowed five dollars from the girl friend and departed for Jamaica. Six weeks later he was dismissed from the island by the Jamaican government for reasons which were a mystery to him. He was returned by air to Toronto and very little is known of what happened to him afterward.

It is known that he returned to his family, but it is not known if he returned to the Canadian police force or what happened to his career as a sculptor.

However, several of the people he met during his adventure did have one brief word from him. He composed a Christmas message, had it mimeographed, and mailed it out to the dancing instructor's girl friend and her family, many of the boat owners he had solicited in Miami, and Mr. Corrington in care of the police station. The message was mainly a variation on the theme of universal love and was grammatically unorthodox. Certain people said that this message indicated that he was deranged, but others said that it indicated only that he was a man who had difficulty in expressing himself in words.

Daisy and the Changes

Tomorrow I went to Daisy's flat and say, "I am miserable, Daisy. All day yesterday. Comfort me." It is dark in her flat but I didn't mind it, because I shall be happy there, in the dark, with the water running like mice all the time in the water closet. It is dry and warm under her blankets with her arms and I shall like to be there forever should she invite me. But as it is I stand ill at ease with my hands in my pockets until yesterday, at which time everything will change—unquestionably for the better. This, at any rate, I used to believe. But now that I shall be old I no longer believed it. This will be a sign of vast maturity on my part and classical wisdom. Daisy desires that we ought to have been married some time ago, in about a month. But she will no longer press this thing after I struck her briskly because she knows I have commitments and it hurt. We have tea and chat and she offered me a chair which I shall take because it matches the wallpaper I am always wanting to buy, though the price would be extreme. It is one thing to be poor but quite another after I was rich. However, I ought not prophesy, because one can simply not see into the past. There are too many unforeseen circumstances which nobody saw even after they happened, so why be smug? Besides, there were better things to think about.

Daisy, for instance. She sat with her legs crossed and I shall see up her dress but I grew sad and pensive before I ever saw because she was old suddenly in a few years, so desperately irrevocably old that I grow weary and bitter to think on it. So I didn't. Instead I rise from my chair to one knee, took her hand in mine and say, "Daisy, I love you. If it is not too late, let us get married seven years ago." "Silly," she says, "I'll be wasted by then. You won't want me." She broke into tears and I have an awful time putting them back together until finally they will be Daisy again. Which they weren't, of course. A woman made of tears, as I knew even at the time, was not the same Daisy. There was nothing to be done. "Look what you've done!" she cried in anguish. "Nothing," I reply. But she paid no mind, because the lines in her face have a conviction of their own. Alas, alas. Here I was, sipping tea with her and chatting, and raising my eyes from the saucer now and then and I had always to be looking into that conviction, which will never do a thing for her face, mark my word, no matter *what* the books may say. This I have always known and now my opinion was confirmed. She had done something to the tea, something unfriendly, doubtless because she doesn't like how I put her back together. I must think about this more deeply and have a smoke, before I went ahead and did anything drastic later.

So I enter the tobacco shop and said, "A pound of coffee, please." But the man behind the counter drew a small pistol from the drawer of the cash register and insisted I had been making fun of him. He will be, however, the last person of whom one could make fun. The pistol will melt in my mouth if he puts it there, so feverish am I. He tells me to get along out, which I was loath to do for I needed a smoke desperately. I beg him for a plug of the most inexpensive coffee and promise him I will pay the day after tomorrow, which is payday where I used to work. But he will have none of this, of course, and asks me instead to sweep the floor, which I do, shoddy though his broom was. Then he personally fills my pipe from his own percolator and would send me on my way, but I am weary suddenly catching a look at his wife and ask him if I may rest for a moment somewhere on her. He mistakes my meaning all too well, however, and will draw out his pistol again; therefore I said nothing and would simply fall in a faint clutching the broom. It ought now to be clear to him that I have had nothing to eat in the way of a woman for ever so long and he will share his wife with me surely. But he didn't, so I rose at once from this immaculate floor and went out into the street where I am wanted.

All in all, between Daisy and the tobacco shop, it was a disappointing day for many years. I knew that I will have to make a change in my luck. So I set out again in spite of the rain and located a shop which carries umbrellas from Spain to Afghanistan. As the proprietor should have been a good friend of mine in elementary school and knew many of my misfortunes intimately, he gave me free of charge not only an umbrella, but a teardrop that will be companionable. What was I to do? I thanked him and took the umbrella and the teardrop, and also I took a vow to repay him when he wasn't looking. This was unnecessary, however, for he already owed me a favor from elementary school which he no longer remembers, what with business expanding all the time in his head like a universe. Therefore in addition to the vow I took an elegant tweed suit, a cashmere topcoat and a pair of shoes.

Thus arrayed I return through the rain to Daisy's. So happy will she be to see me in my new circumstances that she gives me a hug and a child as soon as I have put my foot in the door. Then I become pensive; the train of my thought wound its way through the Rocky Mountains and across the plains to the Pacific Ocean, and out the window I saw the great California coast waving at me like the flag of Freedom itself for one brief moment before the child began to sing. It was a terrible opera, I think, though I am not a connoisseur. Still, we did buy a book of tickets, Daisy and I, and now had an official box for the season, and that ought to entitle us to express our opinion, really, though no mention is made of the fact on the tickets.

The operas vary. Some are grand and some are light. Some are old and some aren't. These are categories I am comfortable with during critical moments in the lobby. The child, however, is inevitably warming up again in the wings before I have categorized the previous act to my satisfaction—the lights begin to blink, the air is anxious, and then, you see, then it is not the child or the opera which is grand or light, but only Daisy. We rush back to our box in the balcony, the light everywhere going dim, the whispers of the ushers in the aisles fading away, and suddenly find ourselves utterly alone, at a great height.

The Burglars

The apartment has been burglarized again. They have taken a record player, a typewriter, a portable radio and other things besides. When I ask the detective if he would recommend a watchdog, he replied, "No, they will only steal the dog as well." And of course, he was right. They did. They took the faithful blue terrier that I had been meaning to purchase for ever so long in spite of the price and for which I could never get up the money until it had vanished from the window of the pet shop. Moreover, the detective dispensed his wisdom modestly, and I will admire him for this one day, but in the meantime I have decided to strike out on my own.

I will have to find them, the burglars. I do not want vengeance, nor do I really care who they were. It is not even important they be stopped; it will eventually be clear that stopping them is not possible in this life, though perhaps it used to be in the next. What is of primary interest to me is that I discover once and for all everything they have taken. If I can discover that, then I will be content.

I will not attempt to inquire further. Into the Why, for example. The Why did not interest me so much. The Why is another story. Or a song perhaps. This is not clear.

Also I would like to know what they will take in the future. Then I can put these things on the doorstep and save them the trouble of climbing the fire escape and breaking the window lock. I like to make life easier for people, specially burglars, because as a class they are universally despised. Anyway they do not burgle because they need the ridiculous objects they take, no more than I myself will need them when I am wiser. What does a burglar need with my typewriter? Did he want to type out the story of his life? I think this is admirable. And it was of great benefit to society that he did, but he didn't, so we are all in the dark still. Yet there he was, lurking in the shadows, laughing to himself. I left the room, shutting the light, and will leave him alone. Now he can take the typewriter without embarrassment to either of us, and begin his autobiography at once. Since I will discover tomorrow, however, that he does not know how to type, has no intention of learning, and moreover that he hasn't even got an autobiography, properly speaking, then I see it was a senseless project from the outset.

Locating the burglars will be difficult. My neighbors are shadowy and none of them are above suspicion, which runs very high in this part of the city, and very deep as well. Not even the dead are above suspicion. Only the angels are above suspicion, my sister says, but then she blushes, because she is delicate and hypersensitive and believes, I think, that she has no right to speak the word angels. Ever since she began the history book that she has given up reading, she came to the conclusion that speaking the word angels will be lewd and symptomatic of a mental disease, and that is why she doesn't mention them anymore in the prayer she tries to remember every night on her knees at the bedside when she thought she was alone.

She occasionally thinks that I too am above suspicion. But I am not above anything as high as that. I have been forgetting myself lately. Many people at work remark on the fact. My supervisor, a frail, nervous, fair-haired youth, will do so increasingly. There is something rude and coarse in my tone when I spoke to him.

"Robert," he said, "you are forgetting yourself!"

I know he is right and I was appalled. Was it I myself who was burglarizing the apartment? I repair to my desk and bury my face in my hands trying to remember. Such a long distance of time will have to be traversed, however, that it takes me the better part of the day; by five o'clock I accomplish nothing, but am paid all the same.

I am often paid "all the same." In the future I will refuse this pay, however, and go hungry in moderation. But my brother, who is a musician, thinks that because I refuse the pay I despise him and everybody. Therefore I told him I will take the pay, after all, and we continued on excellent terms, my brother and I, until today when he suggested that I request a raise in salary. Then I laughed. And as I could see he wanted to be rid of me, I went out into the street where I am wanted.

I am wanted for murder and other petty crimes. No doubt I can fulfill these wants of the street, but won't, and I stand firm on this point even though it has begun to rain and the pedestrians are running in all directions.

In the end it was my downstairs neighbor Evers who found me and drew me indoors. He led me up to the couch in my apartment and brought a cup of hot chocolate. He said I was wet through and through. But this isn't so, as I am dry inside. All the same, I didn't protest, because even though it is good to enter into conversation with him, it is better to enter alone.

He heard about my burglary and gives me excellent advice. He recommends putting a wire across my doorway before bedtime, and razor blades on the bottoms of the windows. I see his idea and will certainly turn it over.

And this I did for a long time after he left. Also I sat by the window. At midnight my brother stopped in to tell me that I had changed. He was worried and grave but I knew he was right. And he too has changed. He has grown thin and I saw him disappear when I shut my eyes. I think it was the music that made him thin. One day he will write a song about nothing and fly away with it and then he will have changed quite perfectly. He is behind on his rent, though, and is unhappy and ashamed. He is unhappy because I have changed, and he is ashamed because he has come again to borrow money. It disconcerts him to borrow money now that we have both changed.

The burglars, however, have no such scruples. They will continue their game no matter how much I change. Even after I change into myself they will continue. Or perhaps not; this is debatable; but with whom will I debate? Occasionally the burglars debate, but they are difficult to pin down and are contradictory and humorous on principle. As soon as I win a point in the discussion and am about to congratulate myself, I discover that something of value is gone again, and the burglars —who but a moment ago were somewhere in the room and debating so amiably—are running off into the night. I go to the window and see them in the distance, climbing the fire escape of the house across the yard.

But of course at this point I grew weary because it became clear that they were nothing, nothing but figures of speech. I crawled into bed and put myself to sleep with a resolution to begin afresh tomorrow and to have no more truck with them.

And I didn't. In the morning light I rose like a king and called everything I saw by its true name.

But it wasn't as easy as it sounds. The true names began to slip out of my mind even before breakfast and I saw last night's resolution in a new light. That I should begin afresh in the morning and have no more truck with burglars was merely a clever lie which would help me fall asleep. When I was a child it was the lie that the light in the corridor will still be on after I shut my eyes which used to help me fall asleep, but now I am wiser and if I want to put one over on myself at night, I have to get up quite early in the morning. So I did. Then I telephone my supervisor to tell him I am sick.

"You have used up all of your sickness, Robert," he replies, "and your job is in danger."

This, however, I have always known, but the danger was never great enough, and he knew this better than I and was very sad. That is why I put the receiver back on the hook gently and sat by the window. All day I sat by the window and looked at my mind and I thought it was like a string of pearls that I had stolen from people whose names I forget unsuccessfully.

In the evening my brother arrives and takes me to a meeting which was held in the apartment of my downstairs neighbor Evers. There is a tremendous crowd of twenty or twenty-five people. They live on the block and I recognize all of them. The meeting is about many things. Mainly it is about how to do away with the burglars. Therefore I wanted to leave but my brother told me that I will be rude to Evers if I leave. I was convinced that he was right, but when I will tell him later that on the other hand I was rude to the burglars if I stay, he won't understand, so I said nothing, which begins to be repetitious, however, and may give my neighbors ideas.

"I don't think you will be able to do away with the burglars," I said at last.

"Maybe not," said Evers, "but it's worth a try, isn't it?"

I didn't answer; I bit my lip because three men will climb in the window and smile. They will take the string of pearls that used to look like my mind and hold it up before the company for ridicule. There was considerable laughter over that. Evers alone didn't laugh, as he is humorless. He looks directly into my eyes in earnest and waits for an answer, so I had to wait with him. Then the three men leave the way they will come and nobody made an effort to stop them. I was glad to be rid of the pearls once and for all. In the morning I would thank the three men but never saw them again.

Then I was pensive. I let Evers wait for the answer alone; I go to the window and hear the meeting at my back. There is talk of sickness, low talk. But I hear it, so I turn around at once and tell everybody that my supervisor has just informed me that I have used up all of my sickness and that they can confirm this fact with him first thing in the morning. They are bewildered and my brother takes me by the arm but I feign a fit of passion and push him away vigorously. This is the only language he and the others understand and they are at once apologetic and timid, much too timid. Also they are sly. They wink at one another and begin speaking to me as if I were a child again. That, however, is wishful thinking on their part and they are deceiving themselves. I don't know how long it took me to get to the door, but when I got there I wanted my sister to take my hand, but she went away with the angels a long time ago. Oh yes, I knew quite well what they are up to, these people. They will have meetings; they will decide to do away with burglars and fail, and fail again, and tell one another they have succeeded. I ran out into the hall casually, so as not to attract much notice and also beg Evers to forgive me for leaving early.

"I have to get up in the morning," I said.

He understood all too well and was deeply hurt. He is a nice man with ugly hands which ruin an otherwise perfect face. He is tall and has a tiny beard. He teaches rapid reading at a rate of pay that insults him, but he has ambition and I predict he will go far afield. I kissed him tenderly on the forehead as I was going up the staircase, but he continues talking in an even voice in his apartment and takes no notice.

By midnight I knew what time it was. I sat in my room in the dark and the meeting continued below. I could hear the words but the floor separated me from what they meant. They were like an opera in a foreign tongue—a grand opera, I think, about murder and other wonders which are easier done than said. I understood everything perfectly. I rose from my chair and began to pace the room and my footsteps fell on deaf ears for a long time, when suddenly I hear that laugh which I knew so well as a child but never heard before.

It comes from the apartment above and I know who it is. We had been passing each other on the stairs for many years without speaking because we didn't want anything to come between us. I know her name from the tag on the mailbox and will bide my time until the meeting broke up below. But then I couldn't hear the laugh anymore because people were talking in the hall. Evers' voice rose above the rest like an eagle and I was glad, glad for him.

My brother came up to see me after they left. I looked at him through the spyhole in my door and he saw my right eye but I saw all of him; also I began to hear the laugh again, so I told him I am asleep. This hurt him, however, and he said he is worried about me. But he isn't; he is worried about my right eye.

"Go home and write a song," I said.

He took my advice and it will be a popular song if it were sung properly.

But it wasn't, so I put on a clean shirt and a simple tie and went upstairs. I stood by her door and hear the laugh. Also I hear her talking softly to her baby whose red carriage I have admired in the street. I think it is good she has him to wake her and laugh with at this hour. I will be glad to laugh with him myself. But things being what they are, I ought not to laugh. It wasn't appropriate. And she herself divined this at once because she is a woman of fine sensibilities and flung open the door which demanded an explanation of me so unexpectedly that to this day I am standing there and looking into her eyes for the just word.

In the end I had to let the open doorway frame an answer. It was like a picture of myself with a flag in my hand. But I knew this was unsatisfactory. We both did. Which is why she felt sorry for me perhaps, and took me in.

Of course, this was my own fault entirely. I had been taken in so many times in the past that I ought really to have been more careful; I think I had been taken in by every trick in the book. And it was an unforgettable book. I read it as a youth and know it like the back of my mind. Truly I had only myself to blame, so I sat in the chair she gave me and told her lies. They are lies about the burglars, though, and may have some foundation.

I told her that I saw the burglars on the fire escape looking through her window. Therefore I had to telephone the police who suggested that I keep her company until help arrives. But as there are too many crimes in the city tonight, help may not arrive till morning. However, I will think twice before I tell her this because her eyes will be speculative. After all, she wasn't an idiot. I saw that at once. She was a woman of insight and humor.

"Why don't you lie down on the sofa," she said, for example.

So I did. Then she brought a little cotton sack filled with ice and put it on my forehead and will draw the window shade against the night.

"Don't," I said. And she knew why at once. She let the window shade be and walked across the room like someone I don't know but would like to, because the hem of her skirt goes to the left as her hips go to the right, and then the hem of her skirt goes to the right as her hips go to the left, and so on and so forth, until she disappeared into the bedroom with the baby.

When she came back without it, she was alone. We both were. And I heard the breathing of her husband in the next room. He will desert her some day a long time ago. I took the bag of ice off my head and went into his room to settle the matter before complications arise. Hannah began to tug at my arm but I told her that I will wake him if she persists and she did. Also the baby began to cry but it wasn't hers. It was mine from a previous marriage on the other side of the street which I ducked out of at the last minute. Then a police car passed and the siren was like the cry of a fish out of water. This will be the signal for the husband to rise. He will rise and walk toward me over the expanse of white linen forever. He will shine and the night will grow calm and I know who he is. He is the ghost of a chance I never took and reminds me of my sister. I began to laugh and he disappears to frighten us by the dark.

Then I took Hannah in my arms to protect her from the fear in my mind but she is proud. She would not stay near me. Looking into my eyes, she put the fingertips of her right hand upon her lower lip and walked backwards like a dancer in the old ballet. This reminded me of Paris, and also Vienna, Salzburg and Odessa, because I had never been to those places. However, I was well-known on the continent, and also admired until the recent misunderstandings.

They were the result of something. I knew this as well as I know myself. Therefore I tell Hannah I must use her telephone at once.

"Everyone is asleep at this hour, Robert," she said.

I will tell her that it is much earlier on the continent but she said she would not let me call the continent because of the expense. This amazed me as I knew the operator would not ask for money, but Hannah said there is a bill at the end of the month. However, I did not believe in the end of the month at the time. Hannah immediately became righteous and said that people who do not believe in the end of the month are excommunicated from the Bell Telephone. This made me blush and I will put my hand forward. I will touch the inside of her left thigh with the fingertips of my right hand and she smiles and let her eyelids drop. Then I will touch her under the ear with the

tip of my tongue because her hair was done up in a ponytail.
She put her left arm between us; it was pointing down; also it
will be stiff at the elbow which was against her belly; her palm
was open and will close around a part of me and hold it gently.
Her mouth makes me think of a pretty little animal in warm
water and I will enter it someday when she kneels before me
and I went into her everywhere at once like three men. Moreover, I am happy to announce that I wept when she lay on the
floor because all her mouths were opening and closing like a
certain season whose name escapes me. This will not be toler-
ated by the authorities, though, because I do not know the
proper name of the season. The authorities will say that I am
sick with prudence. They will say also that I am lying when I
said that I enter her like three men. But they are mistaken.
Because when I say I enter her like three men, I am not lying, I
am singing *Melancholy Baby*.

Hannah told me to be quiet, however, because I may wake
up something. Also she said I had a bad voice and that I wasn't
singing the words right. Anyway she did not like the song to
begin with. She did not say it all straight out, but I knew what
was behind her solicitations and I went back down the stairs. In
fact, I will not go up the stairs in the first place. What is the use,
really, if the whole affair is going to end with insults?

It was dark as usual. Evers was out there now with his gang
and they will join up with the burglars. I will go out and put a
stop to it again and again. Except that the street is too far away
and I could not reason with the distance which lay there stretched
out like a dead man between me and all the bloody work that is
going on.

I have determined nevertheless to be happy. Hannah has told
me that I must, and my sister said that it is a sin to be sad. Also
my brother said that a happy man will change the world.

I see his point. I see it with my naked eye. It is very far away like a great star. However, I have been considering it with unflagging seriousness for so long now that I had forgotten that my brother was the one who originally made it. Perhaps he himself has forgotten. Certainly his behavior lately would indicate that he has. However, I don't put much stock in behavior. Now that Evers has joined up with the burglars, they will be murdering women and children and men of all ages with such astonishing regularity that any behavior is open to question like a wound and should be taken with a grain of salt. I don't like it. In fact, I think it is very deep.

I think many other things as well. I think that I is a most impersonal pronoun and only a figure of speech. I think I is like the burglars and is no more than one of the thinnest letters in the alphabet. I think I reminds me of a hungry man, and I will write ninety-nine cantos about him in an expansive mode. And those of you who design kingdoms will understand what I am speaking about just as clearly as if I had not spoken at all.

I know now that the end is surely coming. It is coming from far away beyond the shadow of a doubt. When it arrives, the last murder will be done. It will be done like a man, in one stroke. Then the burglars will quit. They will drape themselves in black and bring tiger lilies and other ferocious ideas to the place where I lie, and I will rest content. I think my only regret will be that I had but one life to give for my country, because if I had a lot more I would save a couple for myself. In a word, it will be all right. It will be right as rain that never lets up and there will be no more burglary anywhere that I know of.

The Huntley Brinkley Report

They pray to images,
much as if they should talk to houses;
for they do not know the nature of gods and heroes.
                                    —HERACLITUS

The Huntley Brinkley Report

September 2, 1968

Brinkley was not there. He was taking the night off. Yet Huntley was not at all apologetic, and there was no replacement. Huntley presided alone. He did a good job but he had no one to smile at sadly, no one to correct and no one to correct him. If he is obliged to go on alone for too many nights, he will surely go to pieces.

I remember the ad about the father and son. The father put his hand on his head and wrinkled his brow in pain, and the voice of an invisible narrator said that a boy needs a full-time father and that Anacin would help. Then the father took Anacin and suddenly everything was all right. He became a full-time father. This is undeniable because he and his son were smiling at each other at the end.

There was a film of a pretty newswoman from NBC in Vietnam. She stood before a hut in a small village and spoke in a wry, epigrammatic style, like David Brinkley. She said that the Viet Cong had stolen all the equipment out of a little medical center the Americans had built, and that the villagers were now afraid to go to the medical center because they were afraid of Viet Cong reprisals.

Hubert Humphrey marched in the Labor Day Parade in New York. Huntley said that the Democratic presidential candidate usually marches in Detroit on Labor Day but Humphrey broke precedent because some politician from Detroit who was in Detroit was on bad terms with Humphrey. Huntley said that the parade was unattended by vigorous demonstrators because so many New Yorkers leave town on Labor Day.

Richard Nixon, the Republican presidential candidate, did not march with Humphrey but stayed in his hotel, relaxing. And George Wallace, the Third Party candidate, attended a stock car race where he addressed seventy thousand people who liked him very much.

Huntley related an incident in which a white man and a black man were shot and killed. I don't remember if he said they shot each other or were shot at by somebody else or what. However, I do remember that he said they were shot and that he didn't seem too happy about it.

After the Huntley Brinkley Report I visited my friend Leo Fry. Leo is a diligent watcher of television and also reads quite a lot of the newspapers and magazines. Tonight he began to boast that because he has two ugly moles, one on his nose and one on his left earlobe, he understands people who are disfigured by bombs and the like.

"Certainly it is true that your moles are ugly, Leo," I said, "but really they can be removed by a doctor."

However, Leo declared that he will never have them removed. "If I had them removed," he said, "I would feel as though I had betrayed the insulted and injured of this world."

September 3

Brinkley was back on the show tonight. Huntley appeared first and told who he is and represents; then there was a long pause while he looked at the camera, quite helplessly, as though he were unsure if he were to give the news alone again. I was afraid he might weep, but he didn't; he disappeared in time and Brinkley came on. Brinkley was smiling when he told who he is and represents. He had an air of confidence. He must have had a delightful vacation and I was glad, glad for him, and myself and everybody who was watching.

The first thing on the news was an incident in Danang. The Viet Cong had thrown some bombs or rockets at some buildings in a small village. The family of a South Vietnamese police officer was killed, his wife and three children. Huntley-Brinkley had pictures of the old men of the village preparing the dead for burial. The correspondent in Danang said that the dead are prepared by the old men because the Vietnamese believe that old men are made wise by the many years of sorrow they have witnessed and borne. Certainly this is a clever belief. There were films of the children being wrapped in the white funeral cloth in their little coffins, and a close-up of a young man weeping who might have been the father.

The Anacin ad was not on tonight and I was looking for it.

After the funeral there was a film of a tower being built in Danang. Brinkley said that the tower cost twenty thousand dollars and will take about six months to complete. It is to be a monument to the unknown soldiers who died. I believe I detected indignation in Brinkley's tone when he spoke of the expense. He appeared to be suggesting that the money and the time would be better spent on improving the homes of the people.

When Huntley-Brinkley was over, there was a half-hour special on George Wallace. It was a film paid for by the Wallace campaign committee, and as I had never seen him I watched the special.

George Wallace spoke with conviction. He used the word

"communist" in the same way that Stalin used "capitalist," Hitler used "non-Aryan," and my friend Leo sometimes uses the pronoun "them." Also Wallace uses the word instinct in a peculiar way. He said that in the days when *The New York Times* was calling Fidel Castro a modern Robin Hood, all the cabdrivers in Alabama knew by instinct that Fidel Castro was no Robin Hood, but a communist plain and simple. The audience applauded this tribute to the cabdrivers of Alabama, but really I think they were applauding the sovereignty that George Wallace had conferred upon instinct—which, if it exists, is a thing that surely everyone has, and especially everyone who hasn't been educated out of trusting it.

September 4

Brinkley said that the commission on violence set up by President Johnson in June was originally supposed to be a one year commission but that it would probably be permanent; then he smiled at the camera.

Huntley too smiled tonight. This happened at the end of the show. It was his first smile in three days. He took off his glasses and smiled. I didn't feel encouraged by this. And if he persists in smiling—that is, if he carries it too far and makes a habit of it—he will certainly upset the aesthetic and moral equilibrium. When later I made this observation to Leo, he rubbed his eyes and did not answer.

In Prague there was trouble at a monument to which the citizens had brought flowers, and a lot of young people were keeping a vigil there. All this was in commemoration to those Czechs who had been killed when the Russians occupied the country a few weeks ago and I was reminded of the tower I saw yesterday in Vietnam. Some Czech police came and told the young people to disperse because the Russians disapproved of the demonstration. The young people left peacefully and a few minutes later Russian soldiers marched past the monument.

"I have the idea that if I were a Czech citizen now during the Russian occupation," Leo later remarked, "I would feel like a child who has seen his father humiliated in public."

Leo was definitely delighted with himself at having expressed this thought, and in fact he immediately treated himself to a glass of the brandy which he reserved for special occasions.

September 5

A Czech filmmaker, about thirty years old, with a thin youthful beard, was sitting in a coffeehouse and there was something which resembled jazz in the background. Huntley called him an intellectual and this impressed me because I knew that Huntley would never have called an American filmmaker an intellectual. Apparently the coffeehouse was a gathering place for intellectuals and the Russians were closing it down. The filmmaker was quite sad and said he would not go into exile because he thought he could do more toward the liberation of his country if he stayed in it. He made me feel guilty about my desire to travel.

"But maybe if you include Czechoslovakia in your travels," suggested Leo, "your conscience will be appeased."

A bomb exploded in the center of Tel Aviv on a busy street. One person was killed and several were injured. This was not just a border attack but an assault from within. There were films of an angry Israeli mob, and policemen pushing people around. Brinkley said that the Israeli police were arresting every dark-skinned person in the area, even some Jews, many of whom have dark skin. Brinkley leaned quite heavily on the part about the dark skin, and may have been suggesting a connection with the color issue in the United States. He said that many Eastern Jews have dark skin.

Tonight Brinkley declared that there is a war on in the United States between the police and the Negroes.

There was an ad on in the middle. A man was crouched under a bed and looking into the camera and speaking enthusiastically about the bed. He said it was a double bed which could be divided into two single beds and you could have different kinds of mattresses on each of the beds. Also he said that each of the partners in the double bed could have a separate blanket. I thought he had a unique idea—a way of bedfellows being close to one another without having to touch one another.

Recently a group of policemen in civilian clothes beat up a group of Negroes in the Black Panther Party in front of a courthouse in Brooklyn, and tonight there was a short interview with two of the Black Panthers. Leo, who was watching with me, said that one of the Panthers looked like Andy from the old Amos and Andy Show. I think the National Association for the Advancement of Colored People was instrumental in putting an end to the Amos and Andy Show some years ago.

Leo said that he once met some of the Black Panthers and that he sympathized with them but that he couldn't abide them for too long. "Because at bottom," he said, "what they want to do is throw me out of a window."

Both Richard Nixon and Spiro Agnew, the Republican candidates for President and Vice-president, were asked to comment on the charges of police brutality in the riot that occurred in Chicago during the Democratic Convention. I don't know why Nixon and Agnew were asked to comment, and didn't understand their comment anyway. I understood only that they wanted to be careful not to offend anyone, but they did.

September 6

September 6 was last Friday. Today is Monday, and most of what happened on Friday I forgot. However, I recall the nomination of a Mr. Fortas to the Supreme Court. President Johnson nominated him but Congress vetoed the nomination. I never heard of Fortas before. Huntley and Brinkley suggested that since Fortas is a liberal and the mood of the country is conservative, he will probably not get the position.

Also there was a film of a meeting about gun control. The meeting was held somewhere in the South and there were about seven thousand people present. Huntley-Brinkley showed excerpts from some of the speeches. All but one were against gun control. The man who spoke in favor of gun control was greeted by howls of ridicule, but the other speakers were applauded cheerfully.

September 9

Tonight Leo came up a few hours after the news and he looked unhappier than usual. He said he saw Huntley-Brinkley tonight and then watched the Special Report which came right after Huntley-Brinkley and replaced The Monkeys. The Special Report was a film of a news conference that Mayor Daley of Chicago gave to defend the charges of police brutality in the handling of the riots that occurred in Chicago during the Democratic Convention two weeks ago. Mayor Daley said that the mass media twisted the picture and only one side of the issue was presented to the public. He told the newsmen that the police were provoked by the demonstrators who used obscene language and threw oven cleaner and human excrement at the police. After the film an NBC newsman said that sixty demonstrators were still in the hospital and were seriously injured, but that only one policeman was still in the hospital.

Leo said that he liked Mayor Daley, that the mayor seemed to be a good man. Leo said that while he was watching the news conference he sympathized more with the mayor than with the demonstrators. He said he saw in Mayor Daley a man who had experienced the burden of power for many years. But then after the news conference Leo went out because he was bored. He decided he would go and visit Berger and borrow money.

Berger, who lives in the neighborhood and has known Leo for a long time, styles himself a professional revolutionary and has made quite a lot of money recently from a book about social conditions. Leo thinks the book is important, likes Berger quite a lot, and was one of the few people in the neighborhood who didn't throw the obvious irony of Berger's good fortune in Berger's face. Leo told me in fact that he didn't see any inconsistency at all in Berger's position, that Berger was still Berger, and that the richer Berger got the richer the revolution got. And this was hard for him to say, I think, because not only is Leo by nature a very envious person but he is afraid of revolutions.

Anyway tonight he decided he would visit Berger and borrow money. Leo didn't really need money. He merely wanted to amuse himself and pass time. Also he said he thought it might do Berger some good to lend money, because it might ease his conscience about getting rich out of telling stories about social conditions. "You might say I wanted to do him a favor," Leo said. "So I went over to his place, you see, but as soon as he opens the door he says, 'I have company,' and he moves me out on the stoop. 'Can I talk to you for a minute?' I say. 'I can't, I have company,' he says. 'Well, you see,' I say, 'I need to borrow some money.' 'I don't have any money,' he says. And just yesterday he is telling me how he just got fifteen thousand dollars from the movies. So I tell him never mind, that it is okay, and I try to comfort him about having to turn me down. But he interrupts me and tells me about the company again! And I'm thinking to myself: Who is that company he has up there? Is it the Revolution maybe? Yes, probably, and he doesn't want to keep it waiting. That is what I am thinking: he doesn't want to keep the Revolution waiting. And I don't blame him. Also he doesn't want to embarrass the Revolution by introducing me to it, otherwise maybe he might have invited me up to say hello, or maybe even for dinner, or just the dessert maybe. So then, after that I walked around and I thought about Mayor Daley, and I changed my mind about him. I didn't care any more about the burden of power. I was all of a sudden in love with the demonstrators. You see? With the demonstrators! But not with the Revolution. No, I didn't like the Revolution one little bit. And do you know why? Because the Revolution, you see, the Revolution is upstairs this very minute eating dinner at Berger's. Yes, and do you know what it is eating? It is eating the demonstrators. That is my opinion."

After Leo left I couldn't remember the Huntley Brinkley Report very well. I tried to call it up but most of the images were lost. This wasn't entirely Leo's fault, though, because I too had watched the Special on Mayor Daley and it had crowded most of Huntley-Brinkley out of my mind. I kept thinking of the mayor's neck, which is very sad and swollen like a balloon that is bigger than his face and reminds me of a tragedy in five acts by Eugene O'Neill. Also Huntley-Brinkley had shown some excerpts from the news conference with Mayor Daley and I was preoccupied with the idea of having seen parts of the news conference twice, and the second time seemed to be a parody of the first.

I tried frequently during the night to remember the Huntley Brinkley Report but had little success. In the morning though, when I woke up, all at once the images from last night's Huntley Brinkley Report crowded in on me, in exactly the same way that on some mornings certain images from certain dreams crowd in on me.

There were three things mainly: a film about the Czechs, the Huey Newton trial, and an Englishman who made a public stand against policemen.

Huey Newton, who is a leader in the Black Panther Party, was convicted of voluntary manslaughter. I never did understand this case as I have come in in the middle. I don't understand if he says he killed the policeman accidentally or in self-defense or if he says he didn't kill him at all. In any event, the sentence is two to fifteen years in prison and he will appeal to a higher court. Huntley said that the prosecutor had attempted to get a verdict of guilty of murder in the first degree. I liked Huey Newton in the film I saw of him the other day. He had the style of an innocent. This means either that he is in fact innocent, or that he has no scruples, or that he has been punished for nothing so often that he can commit a certain amount of crimes with a clear conscience because they have already been paid for.

Huntley-Brinkley showed films tonight of attractive young Czechs working in rather pleasant orchards and farms and factories and Brinkley said that you could see by these films the effects of Russian oppression.

The show ended in London on Victoria Street. Apparently the government had bought all the property on this block to make room for a new project of some sort, and all the property owners capitulated peacefully but one. He refused to leave his home because it was his home and also he thought the government didn't offer him enough money. He had erected a high barbed-wire fence in front of his property. He and his wife stood behind the fence and shouted defiantly at the police and brandished sticks. Then one of the policemen motioned at a tractor which proceeded to rip up the fence. Then the man climbed up on the tractor and shouted, but the police pulled him down and carried him away together with his wife, who was rather stout and was weeping. There were many sympathetic bystanders cheering the man and wife at the beginning.

Brinkley's final comment was that there was an NBC newsman in London who had been fighting in the courts for twelve years over three feet of his rose garden which the English government had taken when they built a new highway. Then Brinkley said good night and delivered a half-smile which at first made me think that he is the possessor of a melancholy wisdom, but then I had second thoughts.

September 10

President Johnson gave a speech today about courage in Vietnam. He said that his military leaders informed him that a bombing halt would mean military suicide and that if a bombing halt was ordered they would resign their positions. When he concluded that we have to hold fast in Vietnam the audience applauded.

What occasioned the President's speech was a remark that Hubert Humphrey made yesterday. Humphrey, who is not only the nation's Vice-president but now also the Democratic candidate for President, said yesterday that there was a chance that some troops would be brought home before the New Year. This obviously made the President angry, and Humphrey today has had to modify his remark of yesterday. He is in a bad spot; he has taken it upon himself to carry on a campaign against his own administration and defend it at the same time.

"Humphrey is like a tomb in which a whole nation is buried and which bears a cheerful inscription," said Leo. "Do you see? It's not good. It embarrasses the mourners."

September 11

I didn't watch the news tonight because in my eagerness not to miss the very beginning I turned on the Admiral about fifteen minutes early and watched *I Spy*, and I liked it so much that I decided I would watch the whole thing. Twice, though, I turned the channel indicator and looked at the news for a moment. Once I saw Richard Nixon giving a speech and he looked confident.

I Spy is a one-hour serial about the adventures of two spies, one black and the other white. They are a team and quite attractive. Tonight their mission was to persuade a traitor that he had made a mistake and to bring him back to America. The traitor was a famous Negro athlete who had defected to a country which I think was supposed to be Red China. He was an excellent actor. When I first saw him, I was quite disturbed because I thought I knew him, that I had met him somewhere, but I couldn't remember where. But then I remembered that I had seen him in a movie once a few months ago.

At the end of the *I Spy* show he saw that he had made a mistake in defecting and he gave a confessional speech before a group of important diplomats. It was quite dramatic because he had been injected with a typhoid serum by the Red Chinese and he was very weak and had to clutch the lectern for support and speak very slowly.

There was one scene which particularly impressed me. The two American spies were talking to a group of Chinese peasants on the street of a small village, when suddenly four Chinese agents with pistols in their hands appeared in the distance. One of the American spies, so as not to worry the peasants, told them that he was an American movie star and that one of the scenes from the movie was going to be filmed right then. The peasants believed him and were delighted and they applauded and laughed after each of the Chinese agents was killed by the American spies.

This was done quite well and was like an allegory of the Huntley Brinkley Report.

September 12

There were films of policemen trying to control a mob in Oakland. The policemen were young and seemed quite nervous. Each held his club in both hands in front of his chest and tried to push the angry people away. But the policemen must have been aware that they were being watched by the Huntley Brinkley Report because they were trying to give the appearance of being gentle and yet in control, and so they succeeded in neither. In fact, they were quite unhappy.

There was one film of a policeman in an office who spoke directly at the camera. He was about thirty-five years old and had lost most of his hair, which was black. He had a sad puffy face; he was truly melancholy and didn't seem ashamed of the fact. He told the camera that there was a time when civilians would give a policeman help when he asked for it. "But now," he said, "they seem to have the attitude of it's your problem, buddy. It makes me sick."

Hubert Humphrey spoke at a college in Buffalo today and, according to Huntley, conducted himself admirably in the face of militant abuse. But on the film Humphrey looked uneasy, and when there was shouting from a few students in the middle of Humphrey's reply to a question, he raised a forefinger, smiled and said, "Equal time," which is television language.

Richard Nixon spoke somewhere too, and he looked confident. And George Wallace accepted the nomination of the American Party in Texas, but he has had the flu for several weeks and didn't speak very long.

I remember Huntley said a few nights ago that Humphrey was conducting himself with bravado and that Nixon was quite calm and cool, and that the calm and cool attitude proved that Nixon felt he was winning.

September 18

Brinkley announced that George Wallace was on the ballot in fifty states and that no one really knew whether or not he had a chance of winning the election.

On the Murine ad there was a woman bathing and a harpsi-
chord playing. The invisible narrator has a gentle voice, but not
satirically gentle. It is quite authentic. He said that there are two
square inches of the body which we don't usually have to wash
because Nature washes them for us with tears. But now there is
more dirt in the air and less tears. Murine, he said at the end, is
the pure and simple solution to eye pollution.

I also remember the White Owl ad, which gave me chills. An
attractive man is smoking a cigar and walking through a park in
spring. We see his face; he is happy, at peace with the world.
Then a look of wonder appears in his eyes and he stares at
something—it is a creature that is part woman and part white
owl, and quite beautiful. She is peering at him from behind a
tree. Then he blinks and she disappears and a pair of young
lovers appear in her place. He sees the creature again and again
during his walk. Then he leans over the wall of a stone bridge
and looks at his reflection in a brook, and the reflection of the
woman-owl appears beside his own, but when he looks up there
is no woman-owl beside him, only a simple woman, quite beautiful, and they laugh and embrace and go off together happily.

There was a film about St. Louis and the police. We saw a
black man being put in a squad car because he had just stabbed
somebody.

Also there were interviews with people who are not famous.
One of them was an attractive woman whom the newsman
called a militant matron. She was working on a Fourth Party
committee and said that if she had read the newspapers only
every other day, she might have been inclined to vote for
Hubert Humphrey—which meant that Humphrey would say
something she liked one day and then contradict it the succeed-
ing day. A cabdriver was interviewed and he said he would vote
for George Wallace because he, the cabdriver, had been mugged
twice, and also he was often verbally abused by black passen-

gers, and he thought that Wallace would put an end to the muggings and the abuse by increasing the power of the police. I don't remember if he said whether the muggers were white or black. The camera went into his home which he had just bought after working at both a night and a day job for ten years. We saw his wife saying good-bye in the hallway to two children who were on their way to school. The camera took an unfortunate view of his home and showed the family always against a background of bare, gray walls; it was quite dismal.

September 19

Today Huntley said that registration at Columbia University went on in an orderly way and that there were no demonstrations. But yesterday there were films of student protests. A crowd of students broke through a line of policemen and started to push up the steps into a building, but were held back by about five black policemen with clubs. Only one of the black policemen didn't have a club. He wore a short-sleeved shirt and looked about forty years old. He had broad shoulders and was quite bald. He stood in front of the other policemen and was trying to reason with the students. Apparently he had success, perhaps because he was black. The students retreated after a while, and we saw them sitting in a circle on the grass. Huntley said they were planning new strategy. A girl stood in the center of the circle and was talking through a megaphone. We also heard a boy talking through a megaphone. Neither he nor the girl seemed to have any violence in their voices. They seemed to be trying to overcome their embarrassment of megaphones and of the battle cries they were called on to deliver, and I liked them for this, their embarrassment.

Tonight Edward Kennedy spoke in Boston at a rally for Hubert Humphrey, and there was a tremendous crowd. It was

Edward Kennedy's first public appearance since his brother Robert was assassinated a few months ago. Huntley said that the rally was at noon and that it was Humphrey's first big crowd in the campaign. When I looked at Edward Kennedy speaking to the people, I was thinking that he must have been thinking, "These people killed my brother John and my brother Robert, and why should I be here? These people are sick and I am afraid of them." And so, because I was thinking this, I don't remember what he said. When Humphrey got up to speak, a lot of people lifted cardboard signs with protest slogans on them and began to chant, "Stop the war, stop the war, stop the war." Humphrey tried to be nonchalant and smile but he was upset and said finally that the demonstrators were ridiculous, but they kept on. I remember the face of a bearded Negro in the crowd and I saw his lips form the words "Stop the war."

Walter Reuther, who is the president of the AFL-CIO, spoke to a group of men who were union leaders. Reuther said he supported Humphrey, and went on at length about George Wallace. He said George Wallace was a racist who would destroy the country and compared him to Adolf Hitler. The union leaders applauded but Brinkley said that a lot of union members would vote for George Wallace.

Some newsman standing in the out-of-doors somewhere with a microphone around his neck said that the polls showed that Humphrey didn't have a chance of winning the election and that the real contest now was between Richard Nixon and George Wallace.

Just the other day I thought somebody on Huntley-Brinkley said that the polls didn't have any figures on George Wallace. No doubt new polls have been taken very quickly.

There was a picture of ex-President Eisenhower, a big still shot of his head against a black background on the wall to the right of Brinkley or maybe Huntley. Eisenhower was smiling in the picture and looked very deathly. He is convalescing from something and is trying to avoid politics but the doctors keep him posted with a brief summary of the news each day. Brinkley said he thought the news wouldn't be good for Eisenhower, though.

I just remembered something I forgot yesterday—about Perlmutter. There was a man named Perlmutter, from the Anti-Defamation League, and he was talking to a newsman, and talking quite expansively as though he were in a great auditorium, but he was only in a small room. Perlmutter said that it was mainly anti-Semitic elements who were trying to keep Abe Fortas out of the Supreme Court. Perlmutter displayed a collection of magazines which contained anti-Semitic articles about Abe Fortas. Perlmutter said that these articles are of two kinds: overt and disguised, but all dangerous and ugly. In any event, this made me realize that Abe Fortas was a Jew.

I don't know why I forgot Perlmutter yesterday or why I remember him now. But about forgetting what happens on television—I noticed something about this tonight. While I was watching the second story reported on Huntley-Brinkley I tried to remember the first story, but couldn't. I couldn't remember even any of the images from the first story, or anything about it at all.

September 20

Tonight they showed another part of the rally for Hubert Humphrey in Boston yesterday. I don't know why they repeated this; they hardly ever repeat. They didn't show Edward Kennedy this time though. They just showed Hubert Humphrey getting shouted and chanted at by the peace demonstrators. He was quite exasperated, and apparently very few demonstrators have been giving Richard Nixon a hard time.

Leo was watching with me tonight. Leo is employed as a
social worker in the emergency ward of a hospital in Coney
Island. Before the Huntley Brinkley Report began he informed
me of the fact that hundreds of people die every year of bed-
sores in the hospital because there isn't enough staff to make
sure that patients are turned regularly in their beds. And after
the Huntley Brinkley Report was over he informed me of the
fact that Huntley-Brinkley hardly ever mentioned Biafra where
millions of people are being starved to death.

There have been a lot of photographs of the Biafran victims
in the newspapers, and if you walk through Manhattan you
meet a lot of people on street corners handing out similar
photographs free of charge. I know people who have tacked
these photographs on the walls in their living rooms and bedrooms. I didn't understand what Leo was driving at when he
pointed out that Huntley-Brinkley didn't have any films about
Biafra. I think that he meant that Huntley and Brinkley were
cheating the public out of an important experience and also out
of important political knowledge, and that their motive for
cheating was to fool everybody into thinking that the world was
in better shape than it is. I think Leo may be right, but if he is,
Huntley and Brinkley will not succeed in such a cheat, and
certainly this kind of cheat isn't characteristic of them.

There was a long film about a sociological experiment in the
South. It was in a classroom. A sociologist with thin gray hair
and spectacles, about sixty years old, presided over a group of
black and white men who were younger than he. He had a white
man and a black man stand in front of the group and improvise
a play in which the white man would play the role of a black
man, and vice versa. At first the two men giggled like schoolboys, and then they tried to cooperate, but they spoke without
conviction and were bad actors. The black man spoke a few
famous phrases that he had heard from white people, and the

white man spoke a few famous phrases he had heard from black people, and they were both speaking at the same time, so that the phrases were quite inappropriate and I was embarrassed for them. After the play came a general discussion among the whole group, and even then, though now nobody was pretending to be a different color from what he was, everybody spoke unconvincingly and was a bad actor. No doubt a classroom is not a good place for acting; the same people saying the same foolish things in the street will surely be quite convincing.

September 23

There was an image of money, of paper money, being thrown onto a desk, and the narrator's voice said that this money was the contributions to the George Wallace campaign. Also there was an image of a crowd of adolescents with long hair. They were outside in the street and the narrator was talking about them in a soft paternal voice, which was like the voice in the Murine ad.

That is all I saw of Huntley-Brinkley tonight because I got caught up again with *I Spy,* but am resolved to be more faithful in the future. If I am not, I will end up writing about *I Spy* instead, and although that might be an excellent idea, it will betray my first intention. The reason I saw two images of the Huntley Brinkley Report is that out of conscience I turned the channel indicator two times—one of which was during a crucial scene, and I missed the climax of the whole drama. Leo said that I must have turned the channel indicator during the crucial scene because I wanted to punish myself, and then he went on to make a connection between this and my sexual attitudes, about which he has no knowledge. He delivered a stern diagnosis which, I think, will not be taken seriously in this decade.

Tonight the white spy was posing as a tennis player traveling in the Orient and he fell in love with a beautiful girl named Tatia who had come to interview and photograph him for a magazine. The black spy, however, was suspicious of her from the outset and cautioned his partner, but without avail. Soon it was clear to me that Tatia was in fact a Communist spy and that she had just murdered three American spies whom she also had photographed. The white spy still loved her, though, and still wanted to believe in her innocence, even after he had seen Tatia's name printed on the backs of the photographs of the three dead American spies.

And Tatia too was in love. So she and the white spy decided they would go off some place together and give up being spies. But since they were still spies, they had to speak of their plans in subtle hints. They kept looking in each other's eyes and it was the way they looked more than what they said that made you know they were in love and would be faithful to one another.

Unfortunately I missed the crucial scene. I know only that Tatia was taken away at the end by some Oriental policemen, and that the white spy was melancholy. So the black spy tried to cheer him up but wasn't able to.

September 24

Tonight when I was rushing home to catch Huntley-Brinkley, I ran into Leo just as he was going up the steps to his house. He sat down on the stoop and we talked a bit. He said he had heartburn and was afraid that he might be developing a cancer of the stomach, so I couldn't just rush off. When I got home I turned on the Admiral at once and went into the bathroom. I had turned up the volume quite loud and Huntley's voice was portentous, but I couldn't keep my mind on what he was saying because I was passing water. When I came out, there was a dead man on the screen and the commentator was concluding something. I don't know who the dead man was, but he must have been killed because of something important or he surely wouldn't have been on the Huntley Brinkley Report. I saw his head in profile. He had black hair and sunken cheeks and fine features, and reminded me of a certain figure which is supposed to represent Jesus Christ in one of Rembrandt's paintings.

Huntley was alone tonight. Brinkley was alone last night. I don't like this, their being alone so much lately.

There was more about Abe Fortas. Senator Sparkman of Alabama said that Fortas ought to bow out because the controversy surrounding his possible appointment to the Supreme Court would interfere with his duties, should he ever be appointed. I didn't understand this reasoning. Also I kept thinking of poor Perlmutter and of his category "disguised anti-Semitism." I think he will be at home this very minute weeping in front of his television set or making an important phone call. The phone call would be best, but the weeping too may not be entirely useless.

September 25

The *Pueblo* is an American ship which was captured about half a year ago by North Korea, which is a Communist country. The North Koreans maintain that the *Pueblo* was captured in North Korean waters, but the United States maintains that the *Pueblo* never left neutral waters.

Tonight we saw a film of the *Pueblo* crew who are being held captive by the North Korean government, which is awaiting an apology from the United States. The film was made by the North Korean government; Huntley said that it was a technically bad film, and it was. The sound was badly synchronized, so that sometimes I thought the voices may have been dubbed in, but I wasn't sure, because sometimes I read lips and they looked like they were saying what the voice on the sound track was saying a few moments earlier. Each of the prisoners who made a speech said in effect that the North Korean government had treated him well, that he missed America and that America ought to capitulate because the North Koreans were in the right. Each prisoner spoke in a very stilted manner and was clearly delivering a prepared speech. One of the prisoners used the phrase "my baby children" several times, which is a phrase that a person who has learned English out of grammar books and dictionaries might invent. The prisoners were like zombies and I thought of a movie I once saw called *The Manchurian Candidate,* which was about American soldiers who were brainwashed by Chinese Communists.

After the film Huntley said that part of the *Pueblo* film was shown on television the night before, and then all of a sudden Huntley was in a living room sitting in front of a television set. This was a film of Huntley taken the night before. He was sitting in front of a television set and watching the film of the *Pueblo* incident, and beside him was the wife of one of the prisoners—the very same prisoner, in fact, who was speaking in the film on the television set in front of her, which was perhaps a Motorola or a General Electric. Then Huntley asked her what she thought about the film, and she said her husband looked thin, but that this was to be expected because of the kind of diet he was probably getting. She was quite stern. However, perhaps she was only putting on a face for Huntley and Brinkley, and if that is so, I like her, and also I was thinking I would like to make love to her someday before her husband comes home, but I don't know where she lives. She said also that her husband didn't sound like her husband and that he must have been reading a prepared speech—except when he spoke of how he missed his family and his baby children.

Brinkley stood on a hill overlooking a valley in California. He was quite close to the camera and he spoke about the people who lived in the valley. He said they were in the lower middle class income bracket and that their political bias was increasingly conservative. When he said the words "lower middle class income bracket," I was reminded of a line from a story called *Rothschild's Fiddle* by Anton Chekhov, who was a Russian writer. The line was, "Yet it was a perfectly respectable river, and not at all contemptible." Brinkley spoke into a slim microphone and there was no breeze disturbing his hair. I could see past him down into the valley. He was like a dark angel standing there overlooking the valley.

Huntley concluded the show with a story about Mrs. Buxton who has baked breads and pastries for many important people, including Presidents Roosevelt, Truman, Eisenhower, and Kennedy. But now the Department of Food and Drugs has forbid her to sell her baked goods because of legalities. Huntley demonstrated unprecedented indignation about this bureaucratic injustice, and this show of indignation makes me suspicious of the philosophical serenity with which he had a few moments earlier commented on the killings in Vietnam and the murders and riots in Mexico City. He embarrassed me with his indignation and I will not believe in the gravity of Mrs. Buxton's predicament. Even so, maybe she is a very fine person.

September 26

I sat and watched television for another hour after Huntley-Brinkley. But then when I turned the television off, I couldn't remember anything from Huntley-Brinkley. And now it is Friday and I still can't remember. But I remember what I saw afterward. It was a sixty minute program from a series called *Ironside,* the title character of which is a police chief whose legs are paralyzed. He uses a wheelchair that is pushed by a young black man. Ironside was shot by a criminal a year ago and that is how he lost the use of his legs. However, he caught the criminal who shot him.

Tonight Ironside was in the hospital for an examination and as he was coming out, a crime was committed. A masked thief broke into a room where drugs are kept and shot and killed an orderly. The black man who pushes the wheelchair left Ironside on the sidewalk and ran back into the hospital. But the thief came out another door and ran into Ironside's wheelchair. Ironside grabbed the thief, pulled off the mask, and saw the thief's face, but the thief got away. Therefore Ironside was the only eyewitness. The next day the doctor told Ironside that his paralysis might be cured if he had an operation right away, and so he said all right. But the thief who was in league with a nurse tried to kill Ironside in the hospital twice but without success, and he and the nurse in the end were apprehended. But even so, Ironside's operation was a failure.

October 2

Today is a Wednesday. On Monday I returned the Admiral to Leo. He urged me to keep it but I insisted he take it back. He had been quite generous really. When I said a few weeks ago that I needed a television set, he said, "Take mine." And we had just met. I had just moved into this neighborhood.

Leo has a wife who is quite beautiful and perhaps that is why he had no reservations about parting with his Admiral. Yet, perhaps even if he had no wife he may have offered me the Admiral—out of pure generosity—but in that case, I think he would have parted with it less happily. To have no wife and no Admiral is a considerable solitude that only the most generous of men, surely, can bear. I say this without irony.

Leo is not his true name. But he is a true person. I call him

Leo because Leo is the astrological sign under which he was born. He informed me of this fact within five minutes after I had met him. "I was born under the sign of Leo," he said. And the subject of astrology hadn't even come up. I wasn't even interested, in fact. It was actually a quite inappropriate remark. In any event, he is a private person, and I will not give his true name, because Huntley and Brinkley have displeased me so often with their habit of giving true names that I have decided to avoid that habit.

Several years ago Leo was employed for a short period as a writer of advertising copy for magazines and television, and he says that television doesn't affect him as deeply as it affects the general run of people because he is always conscious of the methods by which television manipulates the viewer, especially in the ads. He laughs inauthentically when I tell him how certain ads have moved me; he says that I am putting him on, but I am not. The White Owl ad gives me chills, the Murine ad gives me a sense of peace and joy, the Beautyrest ad makes me laugh and disquiets me, and so on. Besides, I think I divine the effects of television on Leo.

For one thing, he says that reading has lately become difficult for him, that the words seem to fall apart on the page and form visual images unrelated to the content. He talks rapidly and nervously and most of his talk is about people and events which he knows only by way of television—as well as magazines, newspapers and the movies. Also, he says that when he dreams, he usually dreams about a room in which there are no people, not even himself. He is the invisible perceiver of a static, familiar room.

Also he says that the emotion attached to each of his static dreams varies. Sometimes he feels horror, sometimes peace, sometimes discomfort, and so on. That is, the forms of the dreams are usually alike, but the emotional content varies.

I think that maybe Leo dreams the way he does because he

has experienced so many eccentric things on television, so many leaps and rapes and miracles, that he cannot put up with any more of them in his dreams.

However, I think also that Leo may be lying to me about his dream world. I think it is possible even that Leo has a quite conventional dream world—a dream world that looks like some fantastic combination of *I Spy,* the Huntley Brinkley Report, and the White Owl ad. But that will be all right if he is lying to me, and I won't hold it against him. What interests me is only the idea he gave me—the idea of some television watcher, any television watcher, who dreams consistently static dreams.

The main reason this idea interests me is that I have noticed a change in my own dream life. I notice that since I have had the Admiral, I don't dream at all—or at least I don't remember my dreams in the morning. Usually what I remember are images from television programs I saw the previous night, especially when I stay up very late and watch for five and six and seven hours.

I gave the Admiral back to Leo because I needed a rest from it. I had begun to watch it for many hours each night, and the desire to record my impressions dissipated.

October 4

The other night I went out looking for some amusement but didn't find any. I came home about two A.M. It was a Friday. I opened the door of my apartment and flicked the light switch, and over the light switch was a crucifix, nailed to the wall by a red thumbtack. It was a slender silver crucifix made of plastic, the size of my hand. I hurriedly searched my closet and the bathroom, then took the crucifix off the wall and put it in my pocket. I left the apartment at once and went downstairs to the street. I walked by Leo's and there was a light on in his window, so I rang the bell, and his wife Daisy answered. I told her that it was very important that I come in, and when she looked at me with some concern, I was comforted. Leo wasn't home; he was at a bar called the Lion's Den drinking with a certain clique of old friends, as is his habit on Friday nights.

Daisy and I went into the living room and the television was on. She told me at once that she was watching a late movie and that I had come in at a crucial moment in the drama. She wanted me to sit down immediately and be quiet until the next commercial. She said it was a weird suspense movie set in a small town in Ireland and that she was glad I had come over because she was frightened by this movie and had been sitting at the edge of her chair for nearly an hour. But I couldn't wait for the commercial, so edgy was I, and I deliberately avoided looking at the television and didn't sit down as she told me to; instead, I took the silver crucifix out of my pocket and showed it to her and said, "I found this nailed on my wall tonight."

I didn't intend this announcement to be melodramatic but it was, and she put her fingertips to her mouth and drew a quick little breath. So I tried to take up a matter-of-fact tone and told her briefly what had happened. In turn, she told me about the movie on television.

It was about a holy murder in a little Irish town. A young atheist writer had come there to visit and began to speak many kinds of blasphemy in public places. Then a pious old man came and killed the writer. The movie was mainly about the old man and his trial. He claimed that the voice of God had commanded him to kill the atheist writer, and the trial was concerned with deliberating the legitimacy of the old man's claim. Also, during the trial certain letters from people who died a long time ago began to arrive in the town. In short, the movie was well calculated to keep the observer in suspense, and Daisy said that when I first brought out the crucifix she almost passed out, but I think she exaggerates. After she had filled me in on the plot, she insisted I watch the end of the movie with her because she was, in spite of everything, just dying to learn the outcome, but I insisted that we talk, and I took up a seat from which the television wasn't visible, and neither of us ever did learn the outcome.

The crucifix on my wall did not have an image of Christ on it, but rather at the intersection of the cross there was a little circle inside of which was a pair of hands, quite feminine, and held in an attitude of supplication. When I looked at them I at once imagined a woman who was beseeching me to become her lover. But I didn't imagine a specific woman. I had rather a general idea of some poor madwoman who was secretly in love with me, who had taken it into her head to invade my apartment when I was out and who would eventually kill me if I didn't discover her in time. However, I do not like to entertain for long the image of a distracted woman with murder and supernal desires on her mind, and also I didn't want to tell Daisy about such a woman, what with the hour so late and the television playing what it was, so we began to assemble explanations.

My landlady, that is what first occurred to me. She is a profound Catholic and she has a key. Daisy said at once, "Yes, the landlady, of course." But then she became indignant and said that the landlady ought not to be coming into my apartment when I was out and that I ought to tell her so first thing in the morning. I could only agree, and ought to have been comforted that we had hit on a plausible explanation but I wasn't, because even if my landlady was the one who nailed the crucifix to my wall, I had still to discover her intentions, and what her state of mind was when she did this terrible thing. On the one hand, she may have nailed the crucifix to my wall just as simply and matter-of-factly as she would fluff one of the pillows on her sofa—thinking perhaps that she would be doing a good deed by putting a crucifix into the apartment of a nice solitary tenant like myself, that it would stand me in good stead, and that perhaps I should discover by way of it some comfort. On the other hand, she may have entered my apartment trembling, feverish, and full of wildly conflicting desires—she may in fact have been just like the image of the insane woman that I fantasized when I first looked at the hands in the circle. In any event, I ought to see about changing the lock on the door.

I remember that in the course of the talk with Daisy I said that a crucifix frightens me anyway, even when it is in its conventional place above the altar of a church—whereon she looked at me oddly, somewhat suspiciously, and began to cross-examine me. I tried to answer with a gentle humorous tone, to convince her that I was a trustworthy person and that she needn't be afraid, but I didn't altogether succeed, mainly because of the situation—that is, the time of night, the eerie television program, the fact that she was without her husband, the unexpectedness of my visit, and then the combination of these things and a few others.

I remember I told her that when I was a child and first saw the figure of a naked man nailed to the cross in the church I was frightened out of my wits and that though the figure became familiar over the years and its power dissipated in a cloud of words and ideas, still I make an effort to sustain the memory of that first perception.

Let me record something plainly. The crucifix is the image of a man nailed to a cross. People come into a vast room in which that image is of the first importance, and I sometimes think that that image has been set over the altars by the priests as a reminder: "That is what we did to him, even to him, because he didn't behave himself. And he was one of the best of men. So remember, behave yourselves, or we will do it to you too." One understands immediately that these people mean business. It is a persuasive image. But the congregants forget easily enough, the image becomes a part of their daily lives and they no longer feel it necessary to speak, either to themselves or to anyone, about the simple fact of what they are seeing.

That, in effect, was what I told Daisy. Daisy was educated in Catholic schools as a child and declared herself a renegade when she became a woman; she smiled at me and indicated very gently that I certainly had an unusual talent for exaggeration.

Daisy said that if she came home one night and found a crucifix nailed to the wall, she wouldn't be at all terrified, because the crucifix was a familiar object to her, that for her it was part of the ordinary furniture of a home. But what would frighten her would be some completely "irrational" object nailed to the wall—like a glove, for example. If she saw a glove nailed to the wall in her apartment, she would be beside herself. But Leo wouldn't be. She thought that Leo wouldn't be. She said he would probably just laugh and begin to speculate immediately about who put it there—that he would take it as a joke. Then she said that I was afraid probably because I was not a Christian and so didn't see the crucifix too often as a child.

But of course, everything she said affirmed what I had just said and yet she didn't acknowledge this, and so I began to feel some exasperation, and at the same time I tried to contain myself and make my feelings more clear to her, and perhaps I got carried away.

I asked her if she had seen the movie called *Psycho,* which was directed by Alfred Hitchcock, and she said she had, and that it had terrified and offended her and that she disapproved of it altogether. I said that I understood her, and then asked her to imagine a sculpture—of metal, stone, wood or plastic—that would be a representation of the woman in the movie at the moment she was being assaulted by the knife-murderer in the shower. Daisy indicated by a certain look that she was displeased that I was talking about this movie. She said that though she had seen it several years ago, the memory of it still affected her unpleasantly, that it upset and disgusted her. I persisted and told her to imagine the sculptures anyway. I asked her what if millions of these little sculptures, all representing the same subject, were distributed among millions of people and were habitually seen and spoken of everywhere—would she still be so terrified of the image? She said that she saw my point and that she probably wouldn't be so afraid any longer. She said it would be just like the crucifix.

I knew then that I had won my point and I thought I would let it rest, but she then asked to see the crucifix again, so I took it out of my pocket and handed it to her. She looked at it for a moment and said that this was not properly called a crucifix. It was only a simple cross, she said, because it did not in fact have the image of a man crucified on it. She was right, of course, and I felt like an idiot.

It was about four A.M. when she converted the living room sofa into a bed like magic; I went to sleep on it and she went to sleep in her bedroom. I lay awake for a while. I thought about Leo and wondered what he would think when he came home from the Lion's Den and found me asleep in his living room. Will he hit upon an explanation immediately? Will he understand why I am here—a thin, pale non-Christian sleeping fully clothed on the convertible sofa, the light of dawn streaming through the window . . . ? He will be not ecstatically drunk when he arrives. The long subway ride from the city will have sobered him a little. He will be melancholy, preoccupied by a sense of waste. He will have just come out of the subway train and he will be thinking about it—the execrable filth, the sad matinal passengers. His mind will be filled with the opinions he had heard and expressed in the Lion's Den, and the jokes. He will be alone, quite alone, and he will enter an apartment where his wife and children are asleep and where the television set will be off, and even if he turns it on, it will show him no more than a test pattern. But he won't turn it on, because he will be too tired, and because I will be there. I will be asleep only a few yards from the set. He will perhaps look at me and the idea that I may have made advances to his wife will occur to him, but he will dismiss the idea at once. He will say to himself that if I had made advances to his wife, I wouldn't be so foolish as to fall asleep in the living room and let him discover that I had been in his apartment while he was out. He will not be certain of this, but he will declare himself certain, so as to simplify matters. Perhaps for a moment he may entertain the notion that I am dead and will make a weary check to see if I am breathing. Then perhaps he will worry for a moment about his wife and children and go into the bedroom and look at them. He may entertain many other ideas and fantasies, all vaguely and peremptorily, but there are two things which are certain: he will reach no inviolate conclusions, and he will not discover until morning or later the circumstances which brought me here.

In fact, he will be in a situation precisely analogous to my own, except that the invader that Leo discovers will be myself who is made of flesh and blood, while the invader I discovered was made of plastic and thin air.

When I woke up the room was light but Leo and Daisy and the children were sleep. I quickly wrote two notes and laid them face up on the bed.

The first was, "Thanks for putting me up." And the second was, "Think of an Arab who comes home late one night and discovers the Star of David nailed to his wall." Then I went home and paid my landlady a visit.

I knocked on her door and she came out to speak to me in the hall at the foot of the stairway.

I showed her the crucifix—or rather, the cross. "I found it nailed on my wall last night," I said. "Someone must have broken in while I was out."

She wrinkled her brow; then she took the cross out of my hand. "That is Ronald's," she said. "Ronald used to have a lot of these. He must have left it."

Ronald is her son and I had heard about him. He used to live in the apartment I am in now. Leo once told me that Ronald was a rough type but was an expert weaver and had a loom in the apartment. I told my landlady that she misunderstood, that the cross wasn't there when I left the apartment earlier in the evening.

"Then it must have just last night fallen down from the wall and you didn't notice it before," she said.

"No," I said, "it didn't fall down; it was nailed up."

I think she began to reply that it must therefore have fallen up into the wall, but she saw that common sense would be against her, so she blushed and fell silent and I felt pity for her.

However, I wanted to make it clear that I didn't like my apartment to be invaded while I was out. I told her that I was too frightened last night to sleep in the apartment and had to spend the night at a friend's. I told her also that I was frightened anyway of crosses in general—but I ought not to have, because it caused her to glance at me suspiciously; no doubt she thought that I was unbalanced and that I would have to be humored, and I will.

Therefore she broke into a maternal smile and said that I shouldn't be afraid, and that the cross must have been on the wall all along but I hadn't noticed it before. I replied that this was unlikely because it was nailed directly over the light switch and I couldn't have missed it. Also it was nailed by a red thumbtack, bright red. But she held fast to her innocence and I hadn't the heart to press her. Also, I was uncertain. Maybe she was telling the truth and the cross had been there all along.

I passed her several times later in the day in the hall, and each time she smiled, touched my shoulder tenderly and said, "Now don't be afraid. There's nothing to be afraid of."

Which didn't help matters in the least—mainly because I think she may be right. Maybe I am not in danger. In fact, maybe I am not even afraid.

When later I told Leo about the cross and the conversation with Daisy, he said that I am deceiving myself. "You're bored," he said. "So you entertain yourself with mysteries. That is my opinion."

"Is it?"

"It is. Also, allow me to recommend that in the future you refrain from having private conversations of such exquisite intensity with my wife."

October . . .

Today I took the Admiral back from Leo and watched Huntley-Brinkley. I saw an astronaut floating about in a rocket ship and talking into a microphone and answering an interviewer who was on earth. But best of all was George Wallace. He spoke at a rally in California and a lot of young people who were against him attended. They did a wonderful thing. Instead of raising their voices in the accents of protest, as George Wallace had expected them to do, they cheered and applauded quite joyously after every sentence he spoke. Also they held up signs, one of which said, "Wallace is our Guru." He had a lot of trouble in giving his speech. He even shook a forefinger one time and said, "Come on up here, you punk," as though he wanted one of the young people to come up on the stage and participate in a fist fight. So a lot of the fans of George Wallace left the rally early, perhaps because they were embarrassed for him.

October . . .

Tonight a newsman in Oregon said that the three states in the union in which there was the smallest population of Jews, Negroes, Puerto Ricans, Mexicans and other stigmatized minorities, as well as the smallest incidence of poverty, riots in the streets and open collective strife in general—in short, the three most apparently sluggish and idyllic states in the union—were the three states in which there was the most intense mass fear and anxiety, and that this fear and anxiety were expressed by a nearly unanimous public demand for more repressive governmental controls. The newsman said that he thought this fear and anxiety were caused by television mainly, and also newspapers and magazines. He said that what the people in these three states were afraid of was the Unknown. I thought he was right, but the way he said it made me think that he himself wasn't afraid of the Unknown. But of course he may be; I don't know for sure one way or the other.

There was the astronaut again floating around the rocket ship and he showed us how he made his orange juice in a plastic bag. Huntley said that this voyage was going well and that next year for sure we would send a rocket ship up which will fly around the moon a few times and come back. I don't know why they want to come back so quickly. If they are going to go all that way, they ought to land.

Also Humphrey was at a rally and made jokes about Nixon, and Nixon was at a rally and made jokes about Humphrey. But Wallace wasn't on.

Also there was another film from North Korea about the crew of the *Pueblo*. It was a news conference with the prisoners. At the end the captain of the crew stood on a chair and made a speech. Huntley said that this was a dramatic moment, because it was unplanned. But we didn't hear what the captain said, because a narrator's voice came in over the captain's voice and told us what the captain was saying.

The narrator said that the captain said he was disappointed that the American government hadn't made a public apology by now and that the *Pueblo* was in the wrong and the prisoners wanted to be released.

But no, that is not the way it was—because Huntley's voice came in on top of the narrator's voice . . . and it was Huntley, actually, who said that the narrator said that the captain said what I have just said he said. It was confusing and exasperating in the extreme, and though finally it is ridiculous, it is not humorous. The crew of the *Pueblo* were quite thin. They were quite thin and I had a daydream about their wives.

October . . .

Tonight I watched Huntley-Brinkley with Leo in his darkroom where he develops his photographs. He is absurdly serious about his photographs; once he went into a rage when I used the word "hobby" in connection with them. He didn't like the word "hobby" in the least. Also he doesn't like the word "outlet." The darkroom is very small and there are magazines, newspapers, books, nutshells, and all sorts of scraps and odds and ends scattered about.

We have a new arrangement with the Admiral. He decided that he would like to watch it again and requested that I return it. He said that I could come up and watch it every evening when Huntley-Brinkley is on.

An interesting fact has come to light. Leo owns two identical Admirals; one he keeps in the living room, and the other in the darkroom.

He informed me that before he lent me the Admiral, he used to seclude himself with it in his darkroom every night, except Friday. Now that I have returned it, he has resumed his old habits. He says that Daisy and he are "not getting along." There can be no doubt but that I am in the midst of a very peculiar domestic tragedy.

Tonight George Wallace was heckled by three thousand elementary school students.

Hubert Humphrey spoke to a crowd of people whom the camera never looked at, but once he addressed them as mothers. At one point in the speech there was a lot of applause. Then he smiled and took a drink of water, and his eyes were narrow and sinister when they peered out over the rim of the glass at the audience.

Once during the Huntley Brinkley Report, Leo switched the Admiral to another channel, on which the Olympic Games in Mexico City were being televised, and we saw a few minutes of a free-style swimming race, which was quite beautiful.

October . . .

Daisy told me tonight that Huntley has been called on the carpet by the Federal Communications Commission because he expressed an opinion about some issue concerning Australian cattle and he ought not to have done this because he himself owns cattle and his opinion is under suspicion of being prejudiced because this issue will affect his personal bank account. The Federal Communications Commission threatened even NBC with something.

I watched Huntley-Brinkley tonight with Daisy because there

were complications. Leo was in a state when I arrived. He had been developing photographs in his darkroom. He came out into the hall to see who had rung the bell and I was one flight below him and had to look up at him at a curious angle. His eyes were wild and red; he was in a sweat, his hair was awry and matted, and he cried out at me that I ought to telephone before I come over.

I was taken aback, but I replied calmly that I will do so as soon as I get a telephone.

This gave him pause, because he knows that I do not have a telephone, and he looked at me stupidly.

"As it is now," I went on, "I will have to telephone you from somebody else's apartment. And in all fairness, Leo, I ought not to barge in on somebody else either. I mean, I should really telephone them too before I go over and use their telephone."

Leo had undoubtedly forgotten about our new arrangement with the Admiral, and in fact I think he was now only dimly aware of who I was, and even of who he himself was. Leaning over the banister, in wrathful confusion he shouted something which let me know that he was busy developing photographs. "Busy, busy!"

It was clear to me at once that he couldn't let me use the television set in his darkroom this night without ruining the photographs he was developing. Merely his opening the door to call downstairs at me may have ruined the photographs.

I ought to have let well enough alone at that point and gone on my way, but I didn't. I told Leo I wanted to repay him fifty of the one hundred dollars he lent me a few weeks ago. But of course he was in too feverish a state to collect fifty dollars and he began to shout again that he was busy.

Daisy came out on the landing. I suppose she overheard Leo shouting in the hall and she was upset. She said I could come into the living room and watch the other television set which the children were then watching. She said the children hardly ever watched Huntley-Brinkley but it would be all right. However, I couldn't do such a thing to the children in good conscience. I tried to reassure her that there was time still to get to the bar at the corner where they have a fine television set. Then Leo went back into his darkroom and slammed the door.

Daisy trembled. I tried to smile at her. I wanted to give her the fifty dollars and take my leave. But all I had was a hundred dollar bill and I was afraid that if she didn't have fifty dollars in cash for change, she might be annoyed with me for making even the repayment of my debt a financial difficulty for her and Leo. This made me dislike myself while I stood there because I could see what a parasite I was, but then I reflected that parasites are often therapeutic for the host, so I said something cheerful and went upstairs and accepted Daisy's offer to watch Huntley-Brinkley on the children's television set.

The children protested. In the end, however, with an air of sullen indignation they went to their playroom.

Daisy and I were left alone. She said that she didn't ever watch Huntley-Brinkley anymore. She said Huntley-Brinkley got on her nerves because they were like a pair of comedians and a vaudeville team—that Chet Huntley was the sober straight man and David Brinkley was the puckish wiseacre. I laughed and said she had made a wonderful and surprising comparison. This flattered her and she decided she would watch Huntley-Brinkley with me. Also watching was Gatsby, who is a fox terrier. Gatsby was named after the hero of *The Great Gatsby,* which is a novel by F. Scott Fitzgerald, who was an Irish-American writer. The hero of the novel was a Jew named Gatz who changed his name to Gatsby because he thought it sounded American and would therefore help him get ahead in American society. And he did, he did get ahead, but he ended in tragedy. I thought it was a sad book, but the fox terrier kept humping my leg while I was trying to watch Huntley-Brinkley and I knew that he would never get ahead no matter what his name was. Even if his name were changed to Rothschild or Felix Frankfurter, he would never get ahead.

This is a Tuesday, and it was last Friday that I watched Huntley-Brinkley with Daisy, so I am writing about all this four days after it happened. Evidently I remember what was happening around the television better than what was happening on it. I remember at least one thing from the Huntley Brinkley Report though. I remember an image of Marines. They were marching in the rain in Vietnam. There were only three or four of them. They were walking through deep mud and had to lift their legs cautiously. It was an image of weariness and boredom. However, I know that I have other images from that television program in the back of my mind, because only a minute ago I recalled an image from the show, but have now forgot it again. This interests me; it suggests that remembering is like a game of hide-and-seek. An image is revealed for a moment, and if its name and location are not called out at once, it will run off immediately and hide again. However, right now I do not care what the images are. I care only to establish the fact that they are hiding somewhere in the back of my mind, whether I locate them and call them by name or not.

October . . .

For the past five days the polls have indicated that Humphrey is gaining in popularity, and that Nixon and Wallace are losing in popularity, especially Wallace. Last night there were riots in Tokyo by students. A newsman said that the penalty for participating in a riot is six months to fifteen years in prison. The students set fires in a railway station and used a battering ram against a big door in front of some military building where there was a cannon. Also they ran and marched in the streets and had open combat with the police. The newsman said that the demonstrators were Leftists and were protesting against the United States and its participation in the war in Vietnam. The camera was jerking back and forth like a helpless anxious man. However, the rioters and the police were not like the camera.

Huntley and Brinkley have been saying for nearly a week that there have been rumors and indications that the war in Vietnam may soon be over because an understanding will soon be reached at the peace talks which are being held in Paris. I remember that last night when David Brinkley suggested that the war may soon be over, I was disappointed, but I quickly reprimanded myself and told myself that I would be glad if the war would soon be over.

Brinkley concluded with a story about a man who said he had just invented a pill which would annihilate every form of pain. Brinkley said that such a pill would make life uninteresting because nobody would have anything anymore to talk or think about. I think this may be true, however, only for those who are accustomed to that kind of society in which people congregate only to give each other pain. Perhaps Brinkley is afraid that if such a pill were taken by everyone, he would be out of a job. But he won't be. He will have his job still. I want to reassure him of that fact and will write him a letter in which I will say that the reason he believes he will be out of a job is that he believes that news is about suffering and death, but it isn't. News is about something else altogether and the first true news report has yet to be given.

October 23

A lot of black athletes have won a lot of the events in the Olympic Games in Mexico City recently. The two hundred meter relay team were all Negroes. When they went up to receive their medals, the band began to play "The Star-Spangled Banner" and the team was supposed to stand at attention with their arms at their sides. But two of the teammates didn't; each of them wore one black glove on his right hand which he made into a fist and raised in the air and bowed his head. This is the conventional salute of black revolutionaries, and the little black fists in the air against the background of the Olympic Stadium reminded me of the moles on Leo's face. The Olympic Committee was displeased and they ordered the athletes to return to the United States at once.

Leo says that what the Negro athletes were saying with their fists was that even though they were put on a pedestal now like the statues of pagan gods, they were not gods, because gods are those who laugh at history from a great height. Leo says that the athletes did not want to laugh at history and did not believe in the pedestal.

October 24

Days and nights are passing now and I no longer keep track of dates in a strict way. However, I do know today's date. I will try to keep the dates as best I can, but now there are so many images and I have a fear of giving the wrong date and adding to the confusion. And it will be better to give no date at all than to give the wrong date.

Yesterday we saw George Wallace. Evidently he is no longer able to be heard at the rallies. The demonstrators are too loud. I felt pity for him and think I have been taken in by something. All along I had been afraid that he might win the election. But he will not. That is very clear.

I am on a train. I have just been to visit my family in Arlington, which is the city in which is the Arlington Cemetery where the Unknown Soldier and other famous people are buried. Huntley and Brinkley were waiting for me in Arlington and they were the same there as they were in Brooklyn where I began this book.

Across the table is a black man who wears the uniform of a specialist-four in the United States Army. I will not speak to him and will continue to write. We are in the dining car. When the Jumbo Beefburger arrives, I will talk to him.

I think that George Wallace was a clever idea conceived by a social engineer who wants to maintain a quiet nation. Nixon and Humphrey have had little harassment at their rallies. At first Humphrey had a lot of harassment but now he has little. Wallace has all the harassment. He serves a function. He is the scapegoat and meanwhile there is business as usual for the Democrats and Republicans.

I have had my Jumbo Beefburger and have spoken to the soldier. He said he is getting discharged in three months and was a year in Vietnam where he was in combat but didn't fire his rifle. He said he was reading *The Wretched of the Earth* by Franz Fanon, who was a French doctor who went to Africa to comfort the sick and to make his life a song of just desire, but he died young. The soldier said he liked the book and had served on some riot squads in the Army.

He left the dining car before me; later when I was walking back through the train I passed him. He was in a seat by the aisle and he nodded and smiled at me in a friendly way. He has a weekend pass and is on his way to New York City where he will put on civilian clothes because the girls in New York City do not favor men in uniform so much anymore. I hope he will discover great pleasure and joy. His nametag said MacIntosh. If he should ever read this, I want him to know that I hope I meet him again on another train. I liked him because he was happy to be young and had seen a lot of murder in the Army but not as much as I have seen on Huntley-Brinkley. I liked him also because he had carried with him *The Wretched of the Earth* on a weekend pass and had a cheerful smile.

October 25

I will invent a character, an assassin. He will look like my friend Leo. He will have two moles, one on his nose and one on his left earlobe. He will be pale and thin and he will have a bad stomach. He will be standing in the woods of New England with a rifle he has just purchased. It will be autumn like it is now. He will wear a dark heavy overcoat. Steam will pour out of his mouth and he will be alone. He will practice shooting at a target which is nailed to the trunk of a fat maple tree. He will be hatless and shivering and his nose will be running.

October 26

Ever since the night that Leo shouted at me on the stairway I have been watching Huntley-Brinkley on the television set in the bar at the corner.

Tonight Huntley-Brinkley showed a film of a rally for George Wallace in Madison Square Garden, which is in New York City, and he had a great reception. Wallace made fun of and criticized the way in which television had been giving a false picture of his campaign. He was quite witty and he performed a parody of a television director. He told the television cameraman aloud what to photograph and the cameraman who was taking the pictures that I saw obeyed. Most of the audience in Madison Square Garden were delighted and they applauded this performance.

The following morning I saw Daisy wheeling her baby carriage in the street and she said that Leo had attended the Wallace rally and had been hit several times by policemen with clubs and that his back was quite sore. He attended out of a perverse curiosity; he does not like George Wallace. Daisy said that Leo was talking with some black demonstrators when the police took him from behind by surprise.

Run For Your Life was on and I watched it. This is a series which is on once a week. The hero is a man who has been told by doctors that he has only a short time to live. He had some money saved up and so he quit his job as an attorney and he travels and looks for adventures. Tonight's adventure began on a train in the dining car where he met a nun and had a conversation with her. The rest of the adventure was about the consequences which proceeded from this meeting, and in the end it turned out that she was not really a nun but was only masquerading.

On my way to Arlington on the train, I too met a nun and had a conversation with her. She was a clinical psychologist and I asked her if her patients were reticent in revealing the intimate details of their sexual lives. I said that I thought that sensitive patients would be reticent because they would be aware of the fact that she had taken a vow of chastity and they might be afraid of giving her pain. She said that perhaps I was projecting, and I think I was, but I am not sure what I was projecting. She said that listening to the intimate confessions of her patients gave her no pain and that they sensed this and were therefore quite open with her. She said that she was able to channel her energies and that chastity was not a problem for her.

I asked her to consider a hypothetical case. There is a young woman patient who is a profound Catholic and is beaten every day by her husband. The young woman is miserable and does not like to be beaten, but the Church will not grant a divorce. The nun said that she would help the woman understand her situation but would not advise her what to do. But if the woman came to understand her situation, I said, she would leave the Church and get a secular divorce. The nun agreed and smiled, and so I laughed and said that she was a subversive. She agreed to this also, and when I asked her if she believed in the infallibility of the Pope, she said no. She got off the train at Baltimore and I was lonely without her conversation during the rest of the trip.

October 27

The assassin will repeatedly wipe his nose with a red handkerchief. His fingers will be numb and he will wish that he had brought a pair of gloves. The metal of the rifle will be cold and will stick to his flesh. The sky will be gray and there will be frost on the grass. He will be a man of ideas. He will have many ideas, and it is important that his ideas be presented to the reader in a convincing way.

October 31

Tonight will be Halloween, but already some of the smaller children have begun to make the rounds. A group of them have just knocked at my door, crying trick or treat. But I kept very still and did not answer. I had no candy or fruit or pennies to give them but perhaps I will buy something for them before the sun goes down. I wondered if perhaps a beautiful woman had accompanied the children, and therefore I wanted to open the door. I watched from my window as they came out of the front door into the street below, and there was no beautiful woman with them.

November . . .

Soon it will be Election Day. Last night on Huntley-Brinkley we saw the two major candidates for President, and also George Wallace. He spoke of the newspapers and television again with sarcasm. Huntley observed that George Wallace considers the newspapers and television his biggest opponents, even bigger than the other presidential candidates, and this reminded me of a remark that Gay Talese, an American journalist, once made in a television appearance. He said that the President of the United States now has greater power than he ever had before in the history of the nation because the check and balance system provided in the Constitution is no longer effective. Gay Talese said that the most effective check on the President's power is now the press—television, newspapers and radio. However, he said that the press is also becoming increasingly totalitarian and he did not like this. I think he may be right because I watched Huntley-Brinkley last night at a neighbor's and they have a nine-year-old son who watched with me and who said, "He is a second Hitler," as soon as the face of George Wallace appeared on the screen.

There was a riot at one of George Wallace's rallies, and I saw in the middle of it one man hitting another man quite methodically over the back with a folding chair. George Wallace said that he was not a racist and that his supporters should be wary of the distorted picture that television has presented of his campaign. He said that the television cameras always focus on the dissenters who attend his rallies, so that the television audience gets the impression that he is surrounded by hostility, whereas in fact he is surrounded by people who are enthusiastic supporters, and I think this may be true. At the end of the film, Huntley remarked that "violence has been the signature of the Wallace campaign"—therefore even in George Wallace's criticism of the press, the press did manage to have the last word. I think that if Wallace saw tonight's Huntley Brinkley Report, he would have a lump in his throat and feel unappeasable rage.

Hubert Humphrey spoke in New York and he spoke mainly about how important it was for people to vote. He was quite frantic on this point and said that he needs every vote he can get.

I realize now that I have hardly spoke about Nixon in this book. He was on last night and said that he would win the popular vote by a margin of three to five million and that this was certain. He was quite confident. All through the campaign he has had excellent advertisements on television. One of the ads is a film that looks like a documentary. We see in this film many kinds of people—black, white, yellow, workers, housewives, children, etcetera. The camera shows all these people in a favorable light and at attractive angles, and the narrator's voice is paternal and benevolent. He speaks in general terms about the virtues of all of these people and what they do. In the background is a type of music that is popularly associated with hope and progress. It is a slow march in a major key played by a symphonic orchestra. One understands immediately that this is a film that wants to show us that it has great love for the family of man, and Richard Nixon's name is never mentioned by the narrator. At the end of the film, however, the music stops, the narrator is silent, and the word Nixon appears in small white letters against a black background and moves toward us and finally dominates the screen.

November . . .

The problem is that it will be difficult to present the ideas of an assassin to the reader in a convincing way. He cannot speak of his ideas aloud. If he is alone and speaks them aloud, he will seem to be crazy or comic, and if other people are present, they will try to refute the ideas, and even if they do not refute the ideas coherently, they will have at least managed to confuse the ideas and dissipate their force.

Tonight Huntley-Brinkley was repetitious and dull, but at eight o'clock there was a film of President Johnson which was made a few hours earlier. He addressed the nation and told us that he had ordered a halt in the bombing of Vietnam. He spoke for twenty-one minutes. At first I thought he was reading the speech because he kept pausing in peculiar places. But the balls of his eyes did not seem to be moving back and forth; also, the speech was ungrammatical in places and so I concluded that he was not reading the speech. He was a melancholy image. Near the end of the speech he said that he would do everything in his power to lighten the burden of the President-elect between Election Day and the inauguration on January 20, just as his predecessors had lightened his burden. He said this without any ironic inflection, but I laughed even though I was alone. And I liked him at that moment. Three times during the speech the camera looked into his eyes. He seemed to be wearing heavy cosmetics on his face and hair and I thought of Gustave Aschenbach, who was the protagonist of *Death in Venice,* which is a story about an old writer who in the last days of his life falls in love with an exquisite Polish boy in Venice. The story was written by Thomas Mann, who was a German writer.

After President Johnson, I went over to Leo's place to see how he was getting on. Daisy had on a new elegant outfit which made me think of her as an aristocrat. Therefore I did not want to leave at once. I wanted to look at her, at this aristocrat. I wanted to talk to her, and win her away from Leo. Perhaps it would be humorous to say that since I had now surrendered the Admiral to him, in all fairness he ought to have surrendered the aristocrat to me. But this is merely humor and I did not think of it at the time. Nor did I try to win the aristocrat from him. Instead I told him about President Johnson.

I told him that President Johnson had just announced on television that he is calling a halt to the bombing in Vietnam.

Leo said something weary and faintly bitter in reply. Then he said that it wasn't enough that the bombing has been stopped.

This put me off and I forgot about the aristocrat. I wanted to ask Leo if he meant that it wasn't enough for him personally, or for the insulted and injured, or for the whole tribe of the dead, or for humanity in general or for what—but I let it go and said that I was sorry but that was the best news I was able to give at the moment.

Then we both were embarrassed somehow. He laughed rather sadly and touched my shoulder. Then I said good night to him and the aristocrat and went back to my apartment.

I think I know now how Chet Huntley must feel. He must feel that no matter what news he gives, it will never be enough, not for himself or for the people he gives it to. He reminds me of the medium I saw the other night on television in a documentary. She was a fat woman with a double chin. She was conducting a seance, and the spirit of a dead person was speaking through her. Her head was thrust back over the back of the chair. Her eyes were shut and she was sweating profusely. It was apparently painful for her to speak the words which the spirit was breathing into her. One felt quite certainly that the people who were listening to her and had paid her would at the end be dissatisfied.

I have been on a train for five paragraphs now. Sitting opposite me are a man and a woman who are strangers to one another. They are both black and about forty years old and have not spoken though they have been sitting together for over an hour. A moment ago a drunken man passed by us in the aisle. The train conductor was leading him by the arm out of the car, because the drunken man was talking very loud. He was black and when he passed us, the man and woman opposite me exchanged a sad and weary look which was like a worn edition of *The Decline of the West*.

Three minutes after I wrote the above paragraph, the conductor passed through the car. He leaned over the seat of an old man sitting behind me and said, "It's *The Decline of the West,* by Oswald Spengler." The old man replied, *"The Decline of the West,* that's right." Then the conductor went away. This was a coincidence.

November 5

On a distant hilltop the assassin will see five children at play. They will be in silhouette against the sky and a certain idea will pass through him like a song.

November 6

Yesterday was Election Day. This morning Hubert Humphrey conceded his defeat, and Richard Nixon will be our new president. He gave a speech at his campaign headquarters and showed us a piece of embroidery that his daughter had made for him. This made me pensive, and I begin to fear that he does not understand the gravity of his position.

November 10

At twilight the assassin takes his rifle apart and puts it in its case. Then he walks through the woods toward a car which he has borrowed for the day from a neighbor in the city. It is parked by the side of a road nearly half a mile away. Some of the trees will already be bare but many of them will be full of leaves. There will be red leaves and yellow ones, also brown and purple. The assassin looks at the leaves and the trees. He wants to admire them. When he was a boy, he used to look at trees and leaves for hours on end. He remembers those hours quite well and is reminded of a short story by Anton Chekhov, titled *Rothschild's Fiddle,* in which an old coffin maker sits by a river and meditates his past life and the imminence of his death. The river is the image which binds his past and future together. He sits by the river and meditates and makes a silent song in which he finds a melancholy intimation of the meaning of his life. The assassin likes this idea. He thinks it is very deep and luxurious.

November 14

A few nights ago I read from this book to Genevieve and Ambrose, which are not true names. They said they liked being read to, so I was encouraged, but often I had the feeling that they did not understand what I was reading to them. Genevieve said that the Huntley Brinkley Report was her favorite television program. She owns a shop which sells women's clothes which are quite colorful and exotic and Ambrose is a sculptor. They are both about forty years old. They are married and do not have children. They have often said that they are like children themselves and therefore do not enjoy visiting people who have children because then they have to compete with the children for attention. I understand this. When I was done reading, Ambrose was melancholy; he said that because of television almost everyone in the nation has a lot of images of horror in his mind and that it has become more and more difficult to live life joyfully. When I had first arrived at their apartment, which has a magnificent view of Washington Square, they showed me some wonderful color slides a professional photographer made of them in colorful costumes and mock-heroic attitudes.

November 27

The assassin will be in my apartment waiting for me on the night that I discover the crucifix nailed to the wall over the light switch. He will be standing by the window and I won't be afraid when I see him in silhouette across the room because he looks so much like Leo and because I will have been expecting him. I had given him the key perhaps that afternoon because he had no place to sleep tonight. He had just been evicted from his apartment in the city because of certain rumors, some of which he says were true. He hasn't yet informed me what these rumors are but I will not press him because I am confident that he will tell me everything in due time. When I flick the light switch I will discover the crucifix just as I did before, except that now I don't search the closet and run out into the street, because I am not alone. However, I take it off the wall and look inquiringly across the room at my guest. Then I ask him if the crucifix was his idea but he is genuinely bewildered and makes no answer. I glance at the sofa and see that his rifle case is lying there.

Also he has his overcoat on as if he had just entered a moment before, and he had. He had entered just a moment before and had not turned on the light. He knows nothing about the crucifix on the wall.

He smiles and then walks deliberately to the sofa and opens his rifle case. It has three metal latches and they click noisily. From the case he takes a sheaf of paper which he places in the top drawer of my desk. Then he returns to the rifle case, closes it nervously, picks it up by the handle and, carrying it like a briefcase, walks toward me. I am standing near the door, which he opens at once. He steps into the hall, turns to look at me and glances at the plastic crucifix in my hand. The idea that he would like to use this crucifix as a target in rifle practice will occur to him but he dismisses this idea. He merely shrugs his shoulders and smiles at me. Then he goes downstairs and I go and look at the sheaf of paper he has left in the top drawer of the desk. It is a manuscript, a journal which is identical to my own, except that in his journal there is no attempt to invent a character.

December 5

Tonight Chet Huntley and David Brinkley were seated in the same room. I was told by a beautiful woman that Brinkley has recently divorced his wife, left Washington and moved to New York. This means that both Huntley and Brinkley are now in New York, and that they speak in the same room, but they didn't before. When I first began to watch Huntley-Brinkley several months ago, I was not aware that they were in different cities. I thought at first that they were in the same room. However, after a week or so I noticed that at the beginning of every show, Huntley said, "This is Chet Huntley, New York," and Brinkley said, "This is David Brinkley, Washington." I wasn't entirely sure, though, of what New York and Washington were supposed to mean in this context. Two possible meanings occurred to me. Either New York and Washington were supposed to indicate the actual physical locations of Huntley and Brinkley, or they were supposed to indicate something about the kind of news each of the men would tell us about—New York symbolizing the center of domestic news and Washington symbolizing the center of international news, or something like that. And it wasn't until about three weeks had passed that I finally satisfied myself that Huntley and Brinkley were not in the same room and that one was in New York and the other in Washington. But even then, to be perfectly honest, I was never absolutely certain. I knew only that they were never shown sitting together in the same room. They were shown always alone—or rather, almost always; occasionally they were shown together on the screen. However, when they were shown together, there was a thin line dividing the screen in half and I couldn't tell if they were in the same room or not. All that I can say for certain is that the thin line which divided the screen in half suggested to me the idea that Huntley and Brinkley were then being televised by different cameras.

Tonight, however, they were very definitely shown as sitting in the same room and there was no line dividing the screen in half. And this means either that they are in fact both in the same room, or that the television people have come up with a way to get rid of the thin line.

Common sense of course tells me that they are in fact in the same room, and I don't see any use in pursuing the question further. What I do want to know, though, is if David Brinkley's move to New York had anything to do with his divorcing his wife. Also I would like to know if he left his wife so that he could be near Chet Huntley. Frankly I am ill at ease with them tonight. I prefer to think of them as being in different rooms. In fact, I predict that no good will come of this new proximity.

"United States 228, South Vietnam 224, Enemy 2647" was printed in white letters on a black background. The numbers represented the amount of people killed last week in the war. Also there were flags beside the numbers. It reminded me of a football scoreboard. Also there were films of the soldiers. They waded through mud and water, and I kept thinking about the cameraman. The soldiers shot at some huts near a meadow or farm. The narrator's voice was a woman's and she said that there were civilians in the huts, women and children. At the end the narrator herself appeared in the film. She had dark hair and was quite pretty. She wore a combat helmet and spoke into a small microphone which she held in her hand. I think I have seen her in Vietnam before.

The Anacin ad was shabby tonight and different from the one that said that a boy needs a full-time father. Also the White Owl ad was different. A man is climbing a mountain. When he reaches the top the woman-owl is waiting for him. She talks at great length to him and gives him a cigar. He smokes it for a moment, looks at the sky, and when he turns to look at her again, she has vanished. I didn't like it; the woman-owl talked too much. Moreover, a man would be breathless when he first arrived at the top of a mountain and he would not want a cigar at that moment. Perhaps he would want a cigar later though, after he has rested.

President John Kennedy who was assassinated six years ago left a widow who recently married Mr. Onassis, a Greek who is one of the richest men in the world and is about twenty or thirty years older than his wife. Mr. Onassis entered a hospital today. Huntley did not know why. Also Huntley-Brinkley showed a house in New York City which Mr. Onassis might purchase. It used to belong to Theodore Roosevelt. Brinkley said that many of Theodore Roosevelt's hunting trophies were in it, and estimated the price of the house at between half a million and a million dollars. As Brinkley spent so much time on this house tonight, I think he will be disappointed if Mr. Onassis doesn't buy it.

We saw a photograph of Sirhan Sirhan tonight. Sirhan Sirhan allegedly shot and killed Robert Kennedy several months ago. Robert Kennedy was then campaigning for the Democratic presidential nomination. Sirhan has dark hair and dark skin and was born in Jordan. Huntley or Brinkley said that tomorrow Sirhan's trial will begin and that it will probably last about two months. The press will not be admitted into the courtroom but will watch the trial on closed circuit television.

December 10

I missed the first few minutes of the Huntley Brinkley Report. I came in in the middle and found myself observing a film that I didn't at first understand. A man was speaking in a large committee room of some sort. I had never seen his face before and I didn't recognize the room because it was just a large committee room without any unique features. However, I assumed at once that the room was in America and that the speaker was an American, and this proved to be true. Also the few sentences he spoke made very good sense, and I immediately liked him. Those few sentences were the most intelligent sentences I had heard on Huntley-Brinkley since I have been watching. He said that he had been sitting there and listening for a long time to a lot of speakers and that he was astonished at the way all of them used the word "hearsay." He said that they evidently believed that hearsay was an evil thing, and that anyone who depended on hearsay for knowledge was in the hands of the devil. He said that this attitude astonished him because all of civilization depended in large part on hearsay—that most of what we know, we know by way of hearsay. I thought this was true and I couldn't imagine why the other speakers had spoken of hearsay in the way he said they had.

But then the film took an odd turn. The first speaker was answered by another man in the room, and it became clear to me as the second man spoke that the first man, who had spoken so intelligently about hearsay, was appearing before a congressional committee in order to defend the interests of the credit bureaus in the United States.

Evidently the complaint leveled against the credit bureaus was not that the credit bureaus used hearsay, but that they used unreliable hearsay, and that they were invading the privacy of too many citizens, and that in fact the whole business was indecent and was out of hand. So right away I understood that the first speaker had misreported what the other speakers had said, and that, in short, he had demonstrated in front of the whole congressional committee that he himself was an unreliable

source of hearsay. It was a great comedy, in fact, though I admit
I understand this comedy only now after trying to reinvent it.

Mrs. Rose Kennedy gave a speech before a large audience
who greeted her with a standing ovation. She is the mother of
four sons, only one of whom is alive. The first son, Joseph
Kennedy, was killed in battle in the Second World War. The
second son, John Kennedy, who became President of the United
States in 1960, was assassinated in office in 1963. The third
son, Robert Kennedy, was assassinated, allegedly by Sirhan
Sirhan, a few months ago while campaigning for the Democratic
presidential nomination. But the fourth son, Edward Kennedy,
is alive and he is a senator in Massachusetts. He introduced his
mother to the audience and he had a cheerful smile. Mrs. Kennedy expressed a feeling of solidarity with the people in the
audience. She told them that they had wept with the Kennedys
in times of sorrow and rejoiced in times of triumph, but that
was all we heard of her speech. I thought that perhaps Huntley-
Brinkley didn't show any more of her speech because she had a
terrific emotion in her voice and it may have exploded into
anger. I thought that perhaps she may have gnashed her teeth
afterward and pounded on the lectern and cried out at the
people that they were a generation of vipers who were devour-
ing her sons, but then surely Huntley-Brinkley would have
shown this. I think that it is more likely that she maintained a
quiet dignity throughout her speech, perhaps because she knew
that Huntley and Brinkley would be watching her and that they
might speak a wry epigram in judgment on her.

Steve Allen is a comedian. Yesterday he spoke to an old
woman in the audience at the beginning of his television program, which is on at four thirty P.M. in Arlington. She stood up
in her seat by the aisle and a microphone was placed before her
and the camera was on her. She was perhaps about seventy
years old and had an Italian accent and seemed quite bewil-

dered. She said that she had come to the television studio to see a certain handsome television star whose name I forget. I remember the audience laughed at her in a way that put me off and that Steve Allen was condescending and sarcastic when he spoke to her. She said that she had seven sons and that one of them looked like Buddy Hackett, who is a comedian and was seated on the stage at the time. One of her sons was with her and he stood up and told us that he worked as a prop man for CBS and that he was also an opera singer. He was tall, nearly two heads taller than his mother, and quite handsome. He had a muscular face, a grayish-black moustache and a gentle smile. One time, I remember, after the audience had laughed at something his mother had said, he leaned toward the microphone and, smiling quite innocently and cheerfully, assured all of us that she was a very great woman. I believe him, and I think it would have been good if he had begun to sing all of a sudden. Then Steve Allen would have been annoyed and also humiliated. He would have taken a pistol out of his coat pocket and shot the singer. The mother would have begun to scream and the audience would then have loved the singer very much. Then the next day in the newspapers we would have seen a sinister photograph of Steve Allen. His hair would be dark and he would have shadows around his eyes.

A few nights ago, on Tuesday, there was a film about the war in Nigeria. Brinkley said it was an unusual film. It was made by a French correspondent. We saw a white mercenary from Holland who was a company commander in the Biafran Army. He sat at an outdoor table in the jungle answering the correspondent's questions and eating. The commander was bare chested; he was fat and strong and appeared to be enjoying his food. He spoke as he chewed his food and answered the questions in a humorous way that was a gentle form of contempt. He smiled and laughed a lot. He had made it known among the men in his company that he had four thousand dollars in his pocket and he liked to make a joke out of the idea that if he was killed in battle, the person who found his body would be rich. After he ate, the camera went with him into a battle where he was killed. We saw a few soldiers carrying his body. There was a soldier at each arm and each leg and one soldier with an arm around the waist. The body was horizontal and face down and wore no shirt. Someone had taken the four thousand dollars, and so another white commander took out a pistol and threatened the men whom he suspected as the thieves. The commander with the pistol stood on a small embankment above the others and was outlined against the sky. The camera was at the foot of the embankment looking up at him. Brinkley said that the money was recovered in the end. The correspondent also interviewed the commander who had recovered the money from the thieves. He was from South Africa and spoke with an English accent. He said that he was fighting because of his conscience. He said that he believed in the cause, that he liked the people he was fighting for, and that he would go somewhere else and fight when this war was over.

December 26

This afternoon something happened. If it had been filmed by a French correspondent Brinkley might have said it was an unusual film. I was walking down a street a few blocks from where I live. Coming toward me was a man, a very tall thin man who wore a hearing aid. He was carrying two portable television sets wrapped in cotton bedsheets. He had one in each hand and carried them like briefcases. The aerials were sticking up through the bedsheets. He was walking quickly and he seemed nervous.

Suddenly a second man appeared. It was Leo. Leo came

running around a street corner and was obviously in pursuit of the man with the hearing aid. When he had caught up with him, he began talking excitedly and pointing at the television sets. But the man with the hearing aid kept walking.

Leo was all worked up and didn't notice me. As he passed I heard him say, "Just let me look at them for a minute."

"What!" said the man with the hearing aid.

"I said, let me look at them!"

I watched them walk down the street. Leo at last succeeded in stopping the man with the hearing aid and they began to argue. Leo was attempting to pull the bedsheets off the television sets but the man with the hearing aid wouldn't permit it.

I was so happy that this little drama was being performed without any assistance from the Huntley Brinkley Report that I went up to the two men and said, "Wait a minute," which took them off guard and they stopped arguing and looked at me.

Leo was surprised to see me, not altogether pleased in fact, and he scowled.

"Hello, Leo," I said. "What's the trouble?"

He answered that this man, the man with the hearing aid, had just burglarized his apartment.

"I did not!" cried the man with the hearing aid. "These television sets are mine!"

"Then you won't mind if we have a look at them, will you," I said.

But he didn't answer. He lowered his brows, glanced at me in a sullen angry way, contemplated the sidewalk a moment, glanced at me again—and at last he put one of the television sets down. But he kept the other one in hand and began to walk away with it. I caught up with him, though, and made him stop.

He looked at me threateningly. However, I held my ground and he put the second television set down too.

I thought that that concluded the affair but it didn't because he then ran back to the first television set, reached his hand under the bedsheet and pulled out a small object, which was a camera.

"What's that?" said Leo, the color rising in his face. "Is it my camera? I think it's my camera."

"No, it's not yours, it's mine!" cried the man with the hearing aid.

"What!"

"It's mine, I tell you! Why can't you let me alone? What do you want from me? What do you want!" The man with the hearing aid was exasperated and nearly at the point of tears. He began to walk backward cautiously, looking furtively from right to left, and then he turned and broke into a run, clutching the camera to his side. I watched him until he disappeared around the corner at the far end of the street.

Leo was bewildered. He picked up the two television sets and looked about him with profound curiosity. When his gaze fell on me, he gave a little start, widened his eyes and glared at me as if I were a stranger who had just insulted him. I began to speak but he wouldn't listen. He shut his eyes for a moment, inhaled resolutely through his nose, and then without a word walked away in the direction from which he had come.

December 31

I want to say a few more words about the Huntley Brinkley Report because two important things have just happened on it. The *Pueblo* crew was released from North Korea in time to celebrate Christmas with their families, and also three astronauts in a ship called the Apollo 8 made a successful voyage to an orbit around the moon and have returned.

There was a lot about this voyage on television because the

Apollo 8 had a television camera aboard and they transmitted pictures of the earth and the moon and of themselves. Huntley and Brinkley were in the NBC studio commenting on the voyage for several days. One time Brinkley had a telephone call from the Philippine Islands from a person who indignantly said that it is true that Magellan was killed in the Philippine Islands but it is not true that his body was eaten by the natives. Apparently Brinkley or somebody at NBC had referred to Magellan earlier in connection with the Apollo 8 voyage. Brinkley laughed when he told us about this telephone call. He laughed in a way I have never seen him laugh before. He could hardly continue speaking. He had some more information to read to us but he kept breaking into laughter in the middle of sentences and I began to laugh with him. Then we saw Huntley and he too was laughing. Then Huntley and Brinkley disappeared and a blond-haired newsman appeared and tried to give us information and he too kept breaking off in the middle of sentences to laugh.

THE END

THE END